Georgia Hill writes romcoms and historical fiction and is published by One More Chapter, the digital-first imprint of HarperCollins.

She divides her time between the beautiful counties of Herefordshire and Devon and lives with her two beloved spaniels, a husband (also beloved) and a ghost called Zoe. She loves Jane Austen, eats far too much Belgian chocolate and has a passion for *Strictly Come Dancing*.

www.georgiahill.co.uk

 twitter.com/georgiawrites
 facebook.com/georgiahillauthor

Also by Georgia Hill

The Little Book Café Series

The Little Book Café: Tash's Story

The Little Book Café: Emma's Story

The Little Book Café: Amy's Story

(Also available together in a bind-up edition)

The Millie Vanilla's Cupcake Café Series

Spring Beginnings

Summer Loves

Christmas Weddings

(Also available together in a bind-up edition)

The Say it with Sequins Series

The Rumba

The Waltz

The Charleston

(Also available together in a bind-up edition)

Standalones

While I Was Waiting

THE GREAT SUMMER STREET PARTY PART 2

GIs and Ginger Beer

GEORGIA HILL

One More Chapter
a division of HarperCollins*Publishers*
1 London Bridge Street
London SE1 9GF
www.harpercollins.co.uk
HarperCollins*Publishers*
1st Floor, Watermarque Building, Ringsend Road
Dublin 4, Ireland

This paperback edition 2022
1
First published in Great Britain in ebook format
by HarperCollins*Publishers* 2022
Copyright © Georgia Hill 2022
Georgia Hill asserts the moral right to be identified
as the author of this work
A catalogue record of this book is available from the British Library
ISBN: 978-0-00-858650-8

This novel is entirely a work of fiction. The names, characters and incidents portrayed in it are the work of the author's imagination. Any resemblance to actual persons, living or dead, events or localities is entirely coincidental.

Printed and bound in the UK using 100% Renewable Electricity
by CPI Group (UK) Ltd

All rights reserved. No part of this publication may be reproduced, stored in a retrieval system, or transmitted, in any form or by any means, electronic, mechanical, photocopying, recording or otherwise, without the prior permission of the publishers.

For the ADCs. Thank you for the 'Zoom handholding.'

The Berecombe News
A Year of Commemoration
By: Keeley Sharma

Our year of celebration and commemoration continues! I hear our guests from the US can't believe what a warm welcome Berecombe has given them — again! So much so, five are staying on a while longer. We'll have the pleasure of GIs Leonard, Victor, Jessie, Curtis and Norman for this summer's events.

Make sure you book early for the picnic and train ride on the scenic Berecombe Steam Railway as it'll be popular, and we'll remember the sacrifices made on D-Day in a service which is bound to be moving.

Now all we need is some sizzling summer sun!

Chapter One

Petra sank onto the chair with a relieved sigh. She flapped her bright pink apron at her hot face. 'Oh boy, am I glad it's my break. Been manic. I've had the Yummy Mummies in, the Knit and Natter lot and the book group as well, as the bookshop's having a stock-take. Not to mention the tourists are flocking in now it's the season. This is the first time I've been able to sit down since opening.' She pushed a mug of hot chocolate over to Ashley. 'Here you go, girlfriend, just what you need on a cold May morning.' She shivered. 'I wish spring would hurry up and arrive, I could do with some sunshine.'

Ashley sipped and remained silent. Looking around Millie Vanilla's Café, she saw a few mums and toddlers still gathered around several tables put together and the remnants of the book group pretending to discuss their latest read but really catching up on gossip. Berecombe's most notorious pair of pensioners and doyennes of the WI, Beryl and Biddy, caught her gaze and waved. It was cosy in here against the unseasonable chill outside and the windows streamed condensation. No one was braving sitting outside today, let alone on the beach with its crashing waves. Ashley dipped her head and concentrated on an errant marshmallow. It was good to be out for once. Since the row with Eddie, she hadn't felt much like socialising. The furious words that she'd spat out were seared guiltily into her brain. She'd been so hard on him.

Petra stirred her hot chocolate. 'What have you been up to? Hardly seen you around and this the first time you've been into the caff. What have you been up to, girl?' She winked broadly. 'Or maybe it's who you've been up to? How's that delicious hunk of an American, Eddie? Haven't seen much of him either.'

'I've been busy. I've started at the Arts Workshop,' Ashley replied eventually, after deciding what to say. 'Working for Ken Tizzard. I'm only part-time at the moment – in fact, he lets me choose what hours I want to do, so it's pretty perfect. I find it tiring, though. Probably no surprise. I haven't worked for my living for over a year.'

'Well, that's not surprising, considering you're still

getting over your accident. Great that you're working with Ken, though. He's a good bloke. What are you doing there?' She tucked in a stray blonde hair that had escaped her victory roll and settled back to listen. As usual, Petra was rocking a full 1940s look.

'Mostly admin. Sorting applicants for courses, ordering supplies, answering the phone. That sort of thing.'

'And will you do some teaching too? That's what you did before the car accident, right? Teach art.'

'Maybe,' Ashley said guardedly. She didn't add that standing up in front of a class was the last thing she could face. Somewhere, in amongst the crumpled wreckage of her Fiesta, she'd lost the sunny self-confidence she'd always had.

'It all sounds good. Really positive.' Petra grinned. 'But what I really want to nosey in about is all the goss with you and your American. You did a right Cinderella act after the ball. Your big coz Noah and I looked for you for ages.'

'I got a taxi home. Had a bit of a headache.'

'Too much champagne, eh?' Petra dug out a tiny mirror from the depths of her violently red dress and checked her matching lipstick.

'Something like that.'

Beryl and Biddy wandered over to say their goodbyes.

'Ooh, ladies.' Petra slid the mirror back into her pocket and grinned up at them. 'Just the people I need to see. How does a choir sound? A fun choir, nothing serious. Getting together and singing a few favourites. Old and new. Thought I'd use the theatre if we get enough people.' She pulled a face. 'Or here, if there's only a few of us.'

'Sounds right up my alley,' Beryl replied, with her trademark enthusiasm. 'What fun!'

'Mmm. Maybe,' Biddy growled. 'As long as we don't have to sing the rubbish that passes for pop music these days.'

It took more than Biddy to deflate Petra. 'Why not come along to the first session and see for yourself? I suspect you might have a fine voice hiding in there somewhere.'

'If only she would hide it more,' Beryl put in, with a wink.

'Think it's high time for your bus,' Biddy said, her thick eyebrows raised in disdain. 'You don't have time to spare for being a music critic, even if we were the slightest bit interested. Come along, Elvis.' The little black poodle trotted after her obediently, and Beryl followed, grinning.

'Don't you love those two? What a double act.' Petra stared after them for a second and then focused on Ashley with a frown. 'Are you all right, my lovely? You don't seem your usual self.'

Ashley popped a marshmallow into her mouth and chewed disconsolately. 'Petra, you really don't want to know.'

'Is it something to do with Eddie? I thought you and he would be all loved-up now he's back from the States. I mean, anyone with half a brain cell can see you two are made for one another. The sexual tension's off the scale.'

'Yes, Eddie is back from the States,' Ashley blurted, unable to keep it to herself any longer. 'Only trouble is, he's brought with him his ex-girlfriend ... who just happens to be having his baby!'

Chapter Two

Petra sank back on her chair, her mouth hanging open in disbelief. 'Eddie has got a woman pregnant? When? How? I can't believe it!' She did a quick scan of the café to see if anyone needed anything and then leaned in. 'Spill!' she hissed. 'You've got approximately thirty minutes until the lunch rush starts.'

'As to how, probably in the usual way.' Ashley tried – and failed – to keep the bitterness from her voice.

'All right then, when? Just now, when he was in the States?'

Ashley shook her head. 'It happened at Christmas. He's got this –' she corrected herself '– he *had* this on–off girlfriend. He came over here and they split up, but they got together again briefly when he went back home for the holidays.'

'And she got pregnant? Are they still together? If so, he had no right to be making the googly eyes at you.'

Ashley felt a glimmer of a smile. 'No. They split up. He realised there was no future for them when he came here.'

Petra sat back again. 'Interesting,' she said, thoughtfully. 'How on and off was this relationship?'

'From what I can gather, Bree—'

'Brie?'

'The girlfriend.'

'Weird name. Bit cheesy.'

Ashley laughed for the first time in a week. 'It's Bree, as in B-R-E-E, not B-R-I-E, like the French cheese.'

'Just as well, or I'd have to swap allegiance to Camembert.'

Ashley laughed again. 'You're so good for me, Petra.'

'What are girlfriends for? So, go on, how on and off was this thing with the cheesy one?'

'From what Eddie told me, most of their lives. He said he's known her since he was a freshman. What's that? First year of university?'

'No idea. I don't know much about this country's educational system, let alone America's. You know, Eddie's in his mid thirties, easily. It's a long time to be in a dysfunctional relationship.'

'What are you saying?'

'That they've been messing each other about all this time with no commitment.'

'I think it was Bree doing all the messing about. Eddie said he's not proud of being manipulated by her and only saw the situation for what it really was when he came to the UK to work.'

'And he would have liked some commitment?'

'I get that impression. Bree wasn't too happy when he announced he'd be teaching in England, had a hissy fit and stormed out. They tried to work things through at Christmas but Eddie realised it wasn't going to work anymore.'

'And she gets preggers. How convenient.'

'What do you mean?' Ashley stared at Petra.

'If you want my opinion, I reckon she's been yanking his chain all of his adult life and, just when he breaks away, she finds the perfect way to keep him tied to her.' Petra drained her mug, looking triumphant at her analysis. 'Is she the sort to do that, do you think?'

Ashley thought back to the evening at the ball and how Bree had hinted at her condition before even establishing whether Eddie had told her. The glint in her dark eyes... It could have been high spirits, or enjoyment of the night – or it could have been vindictiveness. 'I suppose,' she began, 'she had Eddie exactly where she wanted him for years and, once he ended it, she wants him back.'

'Or maybe not even that. She just wants to carry on playing the mind games.'

'Do you think people really do things like that?'

'Who knows? Nothing would surprise me.' Petra shrugged. 'Maybe the biological clock has struck and she's always had Eddie lined up as her potential baby's father? Then he announces he's going to work abroad. Plan scuppered. Last chance you've got with him, stick a pin in the condom or forget your diaphragm and Bob's your uncle. Or bun's in the oven, if you like. She obviously didn't envisage her doting Eddie falling for a gorgeous Brit. And by that, I mean you, my lovely. That must have ruined her plans even more.'

'The tragedy is, I think if she hadn't messed Eddie around so much, he would've happily settled down with her and had children. He told me he's always wanted kids.'

Petra reached out a hand. 'But he's fallen for you. Anyone can see that.'

'I was beginning to think so.' Ashley sighed. 'I mean, we haven't done much except kiss but, oh God—'

'What?'

'It was electric!' She scanned Petra's expression and felt herself blush. 'There's definitely a physical connection. But besides that, I really felt he was someone I could build a life with. I could see myself growing old with him. Does that sound ridiculous when I barely know the guy?'

'No, girlfriend. I reckon when you know, you know.'

'And now it's all so horribly complicated. And I have to decide whether knowing he's having a baby with his ex is something I can live with.'

Petra glanced over to the till where a customer was waiting to pay. 'Hold that thought; I'll be right back.'

Ashley stared through the steamed-up windows at the churning waves outside. A gull flew low and then caught the edge of a thermal, effortlessly soaring into the sky. Everywhere was grey today. Lowering clouds bulging with rain, sea spray clouding the air, even the sea itself was a furtive-looking greeny-grey. For the first time in days, her fingers itched for her paints and she cursed herself for forgetting her sketch pad.

Staring hard and trying to memorise the scene, she couldn't help but let her thoughts stray to what Petra had said. Was it possible that a woman could be so calculating as to deliberately chance getting pregnant with the man who had finally broken off their relationship? Ashley had never met a truly manipulative person. She'd known a few casually tactless or thoughtless ones, but never anyone who was capable of what Petra suspected of Bree.

Her eye was caught by one of the Yummy Mummies wrestling her little boy into his jacket and failing, as the toddler was having none of it. Maybe Bree had seen it as the last chance to have a baby with a man whom, no matter how dysfunctional the relationship, she knew and trusted? A longing deep inside Ashley bloomed and twisted. She'd love a little boy like the one currently being bundled into his cute mini parka.

She'd always assumed she would have children one day. The accident had changed all that, as it had changed so many things. Pre-accident, she'd been coming up to thirty and in a stable relationship. Marriage and children were vague but promising prospects on the distant horizon. Now all that hung in an uncertain balance. There was no man and, because of her injuries, there might be no children. If Bree had grasped at the chance to have a baby, even if it had been done with deliberate deception, Ashley had a niggle of understanding and some sympathy. How could she not? It still didn't solve the problem of how she felt about the whole situation, though. She sighed.

Petra put an espresso in front of her and a piece of coffee-and-walnut cake. 'On the house. You can't face this sort of problem without cake.' She sat down next to

Ashley and added, more gently, 'So, what are you going to do about Eddie?'

'The last thing he said is that he wants to start a relationship with me.'

'Well, of course he does. He's that sort of man.'

'He told me he was falling in love with me.'

'Wow! But?'

'But how can I go into a relationship with him, knowing Bree is in the background all the time and about to have his baby? A baby he really wants.'

Ashley had a sudden vision of Eddie as a dad. Holding the newborn in his arms with the look of awe and masculine pride that fathers have when they see their child for the first time. 'Oh, Petra, he really wants this baby.' She picked up the coffee cup and swallowed the espresso in one. 'I just don't know if I can share him like this. I don't want to share him at all! He accused me of wanting the fairytale, and maybe I do. I certainly want something as uncomplicated as possible. It's not much to ask, is it?' She pushed the cup away, her lower lip trembling. 'And, if Bree has had this hold over him for so long, what's to say they won't get back together again, especially as she's the mother of his child? How can I compete against that?'

Petra reached for her hand again. 'Girl, this is tough. Yes, it's not an ideal way to start a relationship with somebody, but I suppose you have to ask yourself if the possibility of a future with Eddie is worth the complication that is Cheesy Lady and Mini Babybel.'

Despite the threatening tears, Ashley snorted out a laugh. 'You're very wicked,' she reproved.

'How did you leave it with Eddie? Did this all happen at the ball? I assume that's why you did the disappearing act?'

Ashley nodded. Then winced. 'I told him I might be able to be his friend but there was no way I could consider having any other kind of relationship with him. Then I walked out.'

'Ouch.'

'Ouch indeed.' Ashley forked off a tiny sliver of cake. She didn't really want any but it was delicious, so she ate some more. 'But, with him teaching in Exeter, there's not much chance of him having to come to Berecombe, is there? We can just avoid each other. Until I've sorted how I really feel.'

'Might be the best thing for a while. Let the dust settle.'

'Or maybe the best thing is not to have Eddie McQueen in my life at all.' But, even as she said it, unhappiness tore through her heart. She had the strongest suspicion she'd never again meet another man who was quite like him.

Chapter Three

Working at the Arts Workshop had wiped her out at first, but Ashley was gradually settling into a routine. Ken was understanding and, if she felt too tired, or was in pain, or feeling overwhelmed, he sent her home without question. Occasionally, she flashbacked to the horrifying night of the accident, to the sound of the lorry slamming into her car and to the crushing pain and the splintered life after it, but every time she ventured out without her walking stick felt like a triumph and a huge leap in her recovery. The solicitor kept her up to date about the promised compensation and she knew that, once she received the money, it would free up her choices. For now, though, she was glad she'd found herself, at the suggestion of her cousin, Noah, in this little town of Berecombe. She was even more grateful for the welcome she'd received and the friendships she'd made, including Ken and his funny, full-on wife, Tessa, along with Biddy and Beryl, and Petra at the café. She hadn't realised how much she'd needed this new start, away from all that was pre-accident and belonged to her old life. She was no longer Ashley Lydden, art teacher at a Shropshire academy, coasting along with a boyfriend with whom she had little in common. She wasn't sure who the new Ashley was yet and what she would become, but she knew she was well on the way to becoming her.

The tiny reception office was to one side of the main entrance, just off the central corridor. From the get-go, Ashley felt at home. The smell of oil and linseed and the proximity of creative minds were as familiar and comforting as a warm hug. The huge airy space that Ken used as his studio made her fingers prickle with longing to work on a big canvas, but she contented herself with quick water-colour sketches on location. Ken was happy for her to feel her way into the job, since, as he admitted, on the salary he was paying, he could hardly be a demanding boss. There was the unspoken promise of teaching work when she felt ready but, at the moment, she was content to ease herself into things by answering the phone and dealing with enquiries.

The main problem was getting to and from work. The

Workshop was some way from her flat and too far for her to walk. Noah often gave her a lift and Ken was happy to drop her home afterwards but being dependent on others rankled. Spotting a second-hand sit-up-and-beg ladies' bike for sale had her wondering if she could ride one again. Her balance still wasn't wonderful, but she thought the exercise might be good – and it would solve the commuting issue. She thought she'd check with her consultant first and was searching for his number on her phone, when a polite cough had her looking up and through the hatch in the reception office.

A man stood in front of it. Good-looking. Longish dark hair, scruffy jeans and sweatshirt, and a collection of large canvases bundled together with thick string at his feet. It must be the painter Ken was expecting.

'Hi,' he said, with a sexy smile.

'Hello, you must be Jake. You're here to see Ken, aren't you? This way.' She led him to Ken's studio and introduced him.

'Ace. Thanks, Ashley,' Ken said. 'Why don't you grab us all a coffee and then come and have a look at Jake's work? I think you'll find it interesting.'

She returned ten minutes later, carrying a tray laden with mugs and chocolate digestives, to find the men poring over Jake's paintings, which were propped up on various easels dotted around the room. Putting the tray on Ken's work bench, she joined them. The weather had become much more spring-like lately and, on this Friday morning in May, light was streaming in through the ceiling windows in the studio.

'Wow!' she exclaimed. It was an inadequate word to describe the paintings. 'So, you're a portrait artist?'

'He is,' Ken added. 'And what a portrait artist. They're stunning, aren't they? This one especially.' He gestured to a portrait of an old woman. 'I like to have a go at the odd portrait myself, but this is way out of my league.'

'She's my grandmother,' Jake explained with a soft Cornish burr. 'Getting on for eighty now. She doesn't mind sitting, likes the company, likes to chat while I'm painting.'

Ashley went nearer. She wanted to touch it. The paint was so liberally applied, it was 3-D. The background was a blur hinting at a blue that could only be the Cornish sea and sky, but the old woman's features had been caressed onto the canvas with inches deep of paint, every stroke moulded with love. 'I love how you use colour. These great slabs of blue and white. Do you use a knife?'

'I use anything I can get hold of. Fingers, palette knife, whatevs.' He shrugged.

'You have an astonishing talent, my friend,' Ken said.

Ashley crossed the room to look at another. 'They leap out at you,' she said in awe.

'That's my great-aunt,' Jake explained. 'She's been ill. I like a face that's had a life, that's been through something.'

'I like these self-portraits too.'

Jake shrugged again. 'If I can't get a sitter, I use myself. Not as interesting, though.'

Ashley disagreed. One self-portrait was in semi-shadow which lent it an enigmatic feel. Not highly naturalistic, it wasn't abstract either. Again, the use of colour gave the painting a fresh, bold feel. Jake had emphasised, at the expense of other details, his high-bridged, well-defined nose, his thin face and sensual mouth with its wide bottom lip. If she hadn't already known he was a painter, she would have guessed. Here was a man who searched beneath the surface and found every painful secret. She shivered slightly.

Ken found a couple of paint-smeared chairs and perched on a similarly decrepit wooden stool. He set them up next to the work bench and passed the mugs over to Ashley and Jake. 'I want Jake to display his paintings here. I've got a couple of gallery owners coming who I think might be interested.'

'Sounds great. What have you been doing up to now, Jake?'

'I studied at the Slade a while back, but my career didn't take off.' He pulled a face. 'Think I'm too old-school for the contemporary scene. Not controversial enough. Couldn't afford to stay in London and I missed the sea, so I went home.'

'There are worse places to paint than Cornwall.'

He gave a lazy grin. 'True. I pick up a bit of seasonal work down at the beach at the surf shop and Mum doesn't make me pay rent, so it gives me time to paint but—'

'But you'd like to be better known.'

'He *deserves* to be better known,' Ken said hotly. 'Don't you think? It's all very well being a big fish in a little pond down in Cornwall, but Jake here needs a bigger audience.'

Ashley sipped her coffee thoughtfully. 'I would have thought, with your obvious talent for portraits, you'd have queues of people wanting to sit and offering good money, too.' It was true. In some ways, Jake's work was conventional, almost old-fashioned; it would appeal to anyone wanting a realistic and flattering portrait.

Jake took a biscuit and crunched it, his white teeth shining against his brown face. 'Loads,' he admitted cheerfully. 'All beautiful, groomed-to-an-inch, bored housewives. Trouble is, they're all so Botoxed-up, any expression is gone. Little of anything for me to get my teeth into. Bland face. Bored face. End up with bland, boring paintings.'

'Ah.' Ashley watched as he took another biscuit. He was younger than she'd first thought. Possibly no older than mid-twenties. 'Couldn't you compromise and paint a few of these women, which would give you the money to live and paint someone more interesting?'

'That's what I've been doing. Trouble is, a few of the bored plastics—'

'Plastics?'

'The women,' he explained. 'They started wanting more than a portrait, if you get my drift.'

'No!' Ashley was horrified but Ken and Jake laughed.

'Loads of them, they come down from London for the summer. Live in their Farrow and Ball dolled-up second homes, pricing out the locals – they're bored out of their skulls and looking for distractions. They think they own Cornwall, own us. Think they keep us going with their money. Some of them started to think they bloody owned me.'

'So, you've come to Devon to escape all that, make your name?' Ashley wrinkled her nose. 'Forgive me, but Berecombe doesn't seem much of a platform.'

'Charming,' Ken said indignantly.

'Ken here knows my mum,' Jake explained. 'Said he'd got a couple of names my stuff needs to go in front of, so here I am.' He looked at the older man with something bordering on hero worship. 'And if Ken says that, it's good enough for me.'

Ashley began to get up. 'Well, I wish you all the luck in the world. With talent like yours, you deserve to go far.'

'Cheers.'

She felt his eyes boring into her.

'Ashley, I'd love to paint *you*.'

Swinging back round to face him, she said in astonishment, 'Me? Whatever for?'

'Because you're beautiful. Because you have an interesting face. And I'd like to paint the face that's lived through what gave you that scar.'

Ashley gasped and, in an automatic gesture, flicked her hair over it.

Ken, as if sensing her discomfort, stood up too. 'Lots of good faces for you to paint while you're in Berecombe, my boy. And not many of them too shy to sit.'

Gathering the mugs back onto the tray, Ashley added brightly, 'You could try Beryl and Biddy, for starters. It's just a shame Ruby's left town. She'd make an excellent subject and I can tell you, she's had a life and a half.'

'Oh, didn't I tell you?' Ken added. 'Ruby's coming back. Biddy and Arthur staged an intervention and they're driving up to London to rescue her from her dreadful daughter. She'll be staying with them as of tomorrow. She'll want to start up the memories project again, no doubt.'

Ashley felt almost tearful. 'Oh Ken, that's the best news I've had all week!'

Chapter Four

Ashley parked her new bike in the cycle slots outside the bookshop and made sure she was secured with a padlock. Patting the saddle and admiring the sky-blue paint job, she murmured, 'Don't want to lose you now, Enid.' The consultant had given his blessing with the proviso to stick to short rides and level ground at first, so Ashley had gone ahead and bought the step-through bicycle. It came complete with an enormous basket on the front, and she was besotted.

Noah had bought her the chain and padlock as a present and added a bright blue cycle helmet. 'Safety at all times,' he reproved when, at first, she'd refused to wear it.

Excited, she took off the helmet and shook out her hair as she made her way into the café. She was meeting

Biddy and Ruby for the first time since Ruby's return to Berecombe. She had the handheld recorder in her rucksack, ready in case Ruby wanted to talk; she had so many questions for her. She couldn't believe how much an old woman's wartime memories had obsessed her and was dying to find out more.

Waving as she spotted them sitting in the window, she negotiated the crowded café and slid into a seat. 'Hello, Biddy. Hello, Ruby. It's good to see you both.' On impulse, she leaned over and kissed Ruby's cheek. 'You look really well.'

'Hello, dearie. Could say the same about you. Got roses in your cheeks, you have.'

Ashley shoved her helmet into her rucksack. 'It's lovely out there. Really fresh. Beryl would say it's a real seaside-y day.'

'Beryl says a lot of things, usually nonsense,' Biddy put in.

'That's not true,' Ashley defended, too buoyed up to be scared of Biddy. 'I happen to think she's a dear.'

Biddy snorted but there was a gleam of humour in her eyes. 'I'll admit she has her moments. I've got your usual on order. Will a hot chocolate do you?'

'Lovely.'

Petra brought it over and, instead of returning to the kitchen, edged Ashley over and shared her chair. 'I hear there's a new man in town. And he's smitten as a kitten with our Ashley here.'

Ruby cackled. 'Oh, I've missed this place. Nowhere like it for gossip.'

Ashley groaned. 'You can't breathe in Berecombe without someone knowing about it,' she said feelingly.

'And then telling everyone else,' Ruby added, with a giggle that belied her ninety-one years. 'So, who is he?'

'A painter,' Petra added, before Ashley could say anything. 'Staying with the Tizzards, putting on an exhibition at The Workshop, and he's the Next Big Thing, Ken says. Tall, dreamy blue eyes, long dark hair and not unlike a certain *Poldark* actor.'

'Give over, Petra,' Biddy said. 'He looks nothing like Aidan Turner.'

'How do you know?'

'I bumped into him and Ken on the seafront.' Biddy patted her hair. 'Said he'd like me to sit for him. Said I had a life in my face.'

'Well, that's certainly true.'

'Less of your cheek, thank you, young Petra.'

'Ooh, I loved *Poldark*. Was ever so sad when it finished.' Ruby rubbed her hands together in glee. 'Perhaps he'd like to paint me an' all?'

Ashley looked around at them with affection. A woman in her nineties, an ex-madam and a singer-cum-café-manager wearing a fifties dress patterned with oranges and lemons. A motley crew of friends but friends all the same. She felt her mood truly lift for the first time since the debacle with Eddie. 'I definitely think you should put yourself forward as a subject, Ruby. I think Jake would love to paint you. If anyone's got a life in their face, it's you.'

Ruby frowned. 'Is that supposed to be a compliment, Ashley?' She harrumphed. 'I'll take it as such. When you get to my age, you don't get many.'

'Think he really wants to paint Ashley,' Petra said mischievously. 'Maybe like in *Titanic*. You know, the film?' She added, in an affected voice, '"Paint me like one of your French girls, Jack," or should I say Jake?' She giggled and then sighed as she looked over her shoulder. 'Better go. Customers waiting. Boy, I'll be glad when Zoe's back from university and can help out. The good weather has brought in the tourists.' She stood up, saying, 'Give me a shout if you want anything else,' and hurried off.

'That's Arthur's granddaughter, isn't it?' Ashley asked, stirring her hot chocolate.

'Zoe?' Biddy said. 'Yes, she works here in the holidays. She's at Durham, studying English. Much good it'll do her,' she added sourly. 'Will come out with a debt and not trained to do anything.'

'Stop changing the subject,' Ruby complained. 'I want to know, when I've only been gone a few weeks, why a painter called Jake is lusting after our Ashley here. When I left, that nice Yank was all over her. What's happened to him? What was his name, Eddie something?'

Ashley chased a rivulet of sugar across the bright pink tablecloth with her finger. 'Eddie McQueen. How long have you got, Ruby?'

Ruby pulled a face. 'Not long enough at my age.' She poured herself more tea and broke off a bit of teacake. 'I do love these things, but the raisins get stuck in my teeth something rotten. Has he high-tailed it back to the States?'

'Something like that.' Ashley left a silence, aware that Biddy was watching her keenly. Changing the subject, Ashley asked, 'So Ruby, how did Biddy and Arthur spring you? I thought your daughter had you locked up like Rapunzel?'

Ruby giggled again. 'Serena's gone off on holiday. Tuscany.' She put a dramatic hand to her forehead. 'Said she needed a holiday. Was *entitled* to one.' She tutted. 'Folks my age got a factory fortnight at Southend, and that's if we were lucky.' Her eyebrows rose. 'Put me in a home, she did, while she skedaddled off to Italy!'

'It wasn't quite a home,' Biddy said with a snort. 'It

was an extremely well-appointed nursing home. Specialising in respite care.'

Ruby shuddered. 'Still, they had us all sitting round the lounge in high-rise chairs gawping at each other to see who was going to cop it first.'

'So how did you get out?' Ashley asked.

A cunning expression came over Ruby's face. She reached into her handbag and slid a mobile onto the table. 'I got myself one of these fancy smartphones. Got the young assistant – lovely boy, he was – to order it for me and set it up, then I rang Biddy. "Get me out," I says. "I can't stand no more cabbage and slop!"'

'Which is very unfair,' Biddy said. 'I saw the menu the day we collected you. You were due salmon and new potatoes for lunch, if you'd stayed.'

'Isn't some kind of permission needed?' Ashley said, trying not to laugh.

'Yes, mine!' Ruby said indignantly.

'Arthur rang Serena,' Biddy explained. 'He must have caught her at a good time.'

'Or after too many barrels of Chianti,' Ruby muttered as she slurped tea.

'And,' Biddy continued smoothly, 'when he explained he was a town councillor of the highest possible moral rectitude and would accept full responsibility, she agreed. He also stressed my past life was, well, in the past. He managed to gloss over the erotic novel writing.'

'Wow, it must have been *really* good Chianti,' Ashley said, and they laughed.

'Well, my Arthur can be quite persuasive when he puts his mind to it.'

'It was either cut short her holiday and fly back to sort me out, or leave me be,' Ruby said.

For the first time Ashley felt a twinge of sympathy for Ruby's daughter. She hadn't taken to Serena but it couldn't be easy looking after a woman like Ruby. She probably was entitled to a break. 'So, Ruby, you're back in Berecombe for a while, then?'

'A month or so, lovie. Enough time for me to do your daft recordings for the memories project and for this Jack or Jake, or whatever he's called, to paint me.'

'Strikes me,' Biddy added drily, 'that young Jake is going to have his hands full. What with painting the portraits of half the female population of Berecombe.'

'Maybe he'd like to paint *me* like one of those French girls?' Ruby put in. 'I take it that means in the nuddy? That'd soon cool his ardour.'

They laughed again. Ashley reached over a hand and said tenderly, 'Oh Ruby, it's so good to have you back!'

Chapter Five

'You seem happier,' Noah observed as they shared beer and pizza in her little flat.

May had slipped into June and the evening sky was clinging onto a blue that seemed to be lit from the inside and was dotted with stars. Ashley had left open the window and a salt-soaked breeze and late birdsong floated through.

She let a blackbird gild the night with a song before looking over to her cousin and answering. 'I'm loving working at the Arts Workshop. Don't get me wrong, it's not like teaching, but it's so good to use my brain again. Ken's good fun too. And it's so great to have some kind of routine in my life. I hadn't realised how much I needed it.'

'It's working. You're looking better.'

'Thanks, coz. I feel it, too. Must be all the cycling. I'm really glad I got Enid.' Noah spluttered at the name but she ignored him. 'The consultant said the exercise would build muscle and that would help my balance and stamina.'

'That's great, Ash. You know, you've done amazingly well. A fractured pelvis is no joke. I'm so glad living here is working out for you.'

'All down to you. It was your idea. And you were right. Berecombe must be a magic place or something, as I'm beginning to feel so much stronger. Physically at least.'

'It's the sea air,' he said, adding smugly, 'so Big Coz Noah just has to sort your love life, then.'

'I'm perfectly capable of arranging that for myself, thank you.' She studied him as he lay sprawled in his usual spot on the floor. She was trying to decide what else to say. Apart from the conversation they'd had on the night of the ball, they hadn't mentioned the Eddie situation again. She didn't especially want to revisit it tonight. 'I'm glad Ruby's back,' she contented herself with. 'She makes life fun.'

'And you'll be able to carry on recording her memories.'

'Talk about a one-track mind!'

'That's what makes me so successful.'

Ashley threw a beer cap at him. 'Also, so modest!' She frowned. It was no good. She was going to have to bring up the subject of Eddie.

'Is there a problem? I thought you enjoyed hearing Ruby's stories.'

'I do, and I'm desperate to hear more about her and GI Chet and their baby. I really want to fill in the gaps. Learn more about her life here in Berecombe during the war. That letter she sent me was dynamite.'

'Certainly was. What's the issue then?'

'Just before she said goodbye when I saw her at the café the other day, she insisted that any recording sessions be attended by me and...' Ashley paused. 'Eddie.'

'As she did at the beginning.'

'Yes, except...' Ashley let the sentence hang and there was an awkward silence.

'You've still not talked to him after your argument? I thought as much. I haven't seen him around town at all since the ball.'

Ashley sipped her beer. 'I'm not sure what I'd say to him even if I bumped into him, to be honest.'

'Maybe start the discussion with the possibility that his ex deceived him and got pregnant with his baby deliberately?' Noah caught her shocked look. 'Petra shared her theories with me.'

'Ah. Petra's theories. You two are getting pally.'

'Yeah. I like her. I think she likes me. We had a bit of a dance at the ball. A bit of a kiss. It's nothing serious, though. I don't think she wants anything like that. Unlike you, so stop changing the subject. Why didn't you tell me about all this?'

Ashley shrugged. 'It's only a suspicion Petra has. She thinks Bree has manipulated Eddie all through their relationship and, just when he broke away, found the perfect way to keep him around.' She sighed. 'I'm not feeling too good about it all, to be honest. I stormed off without giving him the chance to explain himself. All I could think about was Bree having his baby. It was all such a shock.'

'Can't have been easy news. I know you wanted children with Piers. Before the accident, I mean.'

'I did, although it might have been a lucky escape with him. Not sure he would have made that good a dad anyway.'

'Whereas Eddie…?'

Ashley sighed again; she couldn't help herself. 'Eddie would make the perfect father. He *will* make the perfect father. Just not of my children.'

'I can see why it all upsets you so much, Ash, I really can, but maybe you should cut the guy some slack? I mean, he could have been divorced or had numerous relationships before you met him. He could have a whole baseball team of babies. None of us are eighteen. We all have history.'

'How would you feel if Petra told you she was having another man's baby?' Ashley countered.

'I get your point, but it's not really the same, is it? Me and Petra are strictly casual. I rather got the feeling you and Eddie were going places. Would be a shame to throw away such potential because of this.' He hitched himself up onto one elbow. 'Besides, I thought you were all prepared to do battle for him. That's what you told me not so long ago.'

'Maybe. Oh, I don't know, Noah – I'm so confused. I don't even know if he's staying in England. For all I know, he'll go back Stateside when his lecturing contract finishes. It's only a temporary one. And now there'll be a child there. Eddie wants to be involved, so I can't see him being happy having an ocean between him and his baby.'

'I know it's a radical idea, but you could always talk to him about it.'

'Don't laugh at me.' Ashley picked off a sliver of pepperoni and examined it.

'I'm not. I'm really not. But here you are, tying yourself into knots about what he said or didn't say to you, what you want to say to him, what you need to ask him. Just seems to me there's a simple solution: you talk to the bloke.'

The blackbird outside was now cackling a warning. 'Not sure I could face him.'

'Well, if Ruby wants both of you at the recordings, you may have to. You know, I wouldn't put it past her to have engineered this situation out of plain mischief.'

'Or misguided matchmaking.' Ashley chewed the pepperoni and swallowed. 'Now you'd know all about that, wouldn't you?'

Noah put up his hands. *'Touché.* Have to confess to pushing you together. I really thought you suited one another. And you've got to admit, he's in a different league to Piers,' he said.

'Piers who?' Ashley pulled a face at her cousin. 'And I don't suppose you'd mind having a renowned historian in the family?'

'World-renowned, more like.'

'He's that famous, is he?'

'In my humble circles, yes. I'm only the director of a small museum, but he's done telly – which, for a historian, is fame indeed.'

'Blimey. I hadn't realised.'

Noah laughed. 'Does it change things?' He folded the lid of his pizza box down.

'Not for me, no.' Ashley sipped her beer thoughtfully.

It didn't. Although it revealed an unknown aspect of Eddie, he was still the same thoughtful, intelligent, funny man she'd got to know. And had let go. She bit her lip. Was he worth the inevitable hassle that Bree and the baby would cause? She simply didn't know. It was completely uncharted territory for her.

'If you're wondering if he's worth it,' her cousin said, reading her mind, 'maybe you should go and find out. It can't hurt to talk to him.'

'I don't have any way of contacting him,' Ashley said stiffly, not wanting to make the decision. Not wanting to give in.

'Ah, but I do.' Noah pulled his mobile from his shirt pocket with a flourish. 'When do you want to schedule the next living memories recording session with Ruby?'

Chapter Six

On Saturday morning Ashley arrived early at the café. She was jittery with nerves so decided on a pot of tea. She didn't really want anything, but it would give her something to do with her hands.

She sat in the window and saw him walking along the promenade before he spotted her. Tall, athletic, with a long stride, his light brown hair gleamed to blond in the sunshine. He wore jeans and a hoodie and had his hands thrust in the front pocket. Her heart flipped over. Why couldn't it all be simple?

Petra had done them a favour and opened up early, saying it would be busy and noisy later. Ashley wasn't sure how much longer they could carry on using the café. Lovely though it was to hold the recording sessions over tea and cake, it was going to become impractical as the town got busier with tourists. She was hoping Ken would let them use the Arts Workshop. Fiddling with her phone, she pretended not to notice Eddie until he was standing at the table.

'Hi, Ashley,' he said softly. 'It's good to see you again.' He gestured to a chair. 'May I?'

'Of course.' Ashley couldn't break out of the awkwardness that was stifling her. 'Would you like… erm… would you like some tea?'

'Petra's bringing me over a coffee. I've missed the coffee here. Best this side of the Atlantic.'

Ashley had missed the way he said the word. *Korfee*. She remembered how his lips had felt on hers, the heat seared onto her skin by his hands. For a second, she couldn't breathe. Then she remembered Bree. And their baby. As Petra served them, leaving a fresh pot of tea for her, Ashley forced herself to get a grip. Pouring another cup of tea that she didn't want but needed desperately, she added milk with a shaking hand. 'How have you been?'

'Good. Busy at work.' He glanced at her before adding, 'It helps. I hear you've begun working at the Arts Workshop. That's really great, Ashley.'

'Thank you. Yes, I enjoy it. It's interesting. We're putting on an exhibition of an exciting new painter soon.

A portrait artist.' She nearly invited Eddie to the opening but stopped herself.

'Cool.' When she remained silent, he sipped his flat white. 'So, Ruby wants us both at the recordings, have I got this right? That's what Noah said.'

Ashley couldn't help but stare at his hands. Long-fingered and suntanned, with immaculately groomed oval nails; they were incredibly sexy. She couldn't understand why she hadn't noticed them before.

'Ashley?'

She shook her head, forcing herself to concentrate. 'Sorry. Yes.' She grimaced. 'Ruby insisted.'

'She's back in town then?'

'Biddy and Arthur broke her free from the respite home she'd been put into.' Ashley breathed a little more easily. Perhaps this was going to be possible after all. 'Serena's in Italy on holiday.'

Eddie shrugged. 'No loss there, then.'

'I agree. We might get Ruby to talk a little more freely in her absence. Did you get a chance to talk to any of the guest GIs about your grandfather?'

'Yeah, I did actually. Had a long conversation with Victor. He was amazing. Told me stuff about D-Day that'll live with me awhile. The memories are seared into him. Ninety-five years old and it could have happened yesterday.' He frowned, staring into the distance. 'Those men went through hell. I mean, it's one thing to study it as history, as an academic subject, it's a whole other ball game to listen to someone who was there describe it. I'm not surprised Grandpa wanted to put it behind him.'

He looked so lost, Ashley yearned to reach out to him, to hold him to her. 'Did he know your grandfather?'

'No.' It came out on a long note of regret. 'Turns out the good old US Army maintained the colour segregation from home. Kept the black and white soldiers separate.'

'Ruby mentioned something about that.'

'Victor was sent over before the white troops. He was in charge of setting up the camp at the top of the hill. The men were billeted there, with the officers in hotels and guest lodges down here in town.'

'Was your grandfather an officer?'

Eddie shook his head. 'Not as far as I know. Just an ordinary GI Joe.'

There was an awkward pause. Ashley filled it by saying, 'That's a shame. But don't give up hope. I'm sure you'll find out about your grandfather soon.'

'Thanks.'

Ashley felt bereft by not being able to reach out to him, to give him some comfort. She changed the subject. 'Noah said you'd done some television work?' she said brightly. 'You didn't mention that when we went to the *Focus Southwest* studios.'

'It was your day, Ash. As I seem to remember, you had enough to think about as it was.'

She gulped. He was so kind. She met his gaze and wondered just what she thought she was doing in rejecting him.

They were interrupted by Biddy bringing Ruby in. 'Ah, there you are, young Ashley.' She nodded coolly to Eddie. 'Do you mind if I leave Ruby here and join you later? Need to get to the fabric shop for some material to make some more bunting.'

She'd gone before Ashley could ask where the extra bunting was going to go. There was hardly an inch of space spare in the café.

'It's for the Arts Workshop,' Ruby explained as she sat down and made herself comfortable, pulling her pastel pink cardigan around her. 'Biddy promised Ken she'd do some. Dab hand with a needle, is Biddy.' She giggled. 'I've been reading one of her naughty books. Darcey Spice is her writing name. It's ever so good. Nice bit of plot to go with all the sexy stuff.'

Eddie choked on the dregs of his coffee. 'I'll go get another,' he said when he'd recovered. 'What can I get you Ruby? Tea?'

'And a teacake, ta. Lots of butter.'

'Anything more for you, Ashley?'

'No thanks. I'm on my second pot.'

After he'd left the table, Ruby leaned nearer to Ashley. 'Still nice-looking, ain't he? Don't know what it is with these Yank fellas, but they got something. Think it's the teeth.' She sucked her own and looked sly. 'You two sorting yourselves out?' When no answer came, she continued: 'I heard the news, lovie. Got a bun in someone else's oven, has he? So what if he's got a baby on the way? Won't be the first man to have messed up. Won't be the last, neither.' Her lips pursed and she added, bitterly, 'Or woman, as we know.' She put her bird-like hand on top of Ashley's. It felt warm and dry and weighed nothing. 'Don't let it stop you being happy, dearie. There's not much of it to grab hold of in the world.' Changing tack as Eddie returned, bringing a tray of tea, she added, 'Ooh lovely, a nice big pot of tea. Like a cup, would you, Ashley, love?'

Ashley thought she'd drown if she drank any more tea, so shook her head. Everyone was conspiring to get her back together with Eddie. But how could she? Bree loomed large in the background like Banquo at the feast. How was she going to get past this? She glanced at Eddie as he sat down and charmingly placed the pot and milk jug with the handles facing Ruby so she could easily reach them. Ashley knew she needed to try, for this kind, thoughtful man who had captured her heart. Trying to focus on why they were all there, she switched on the handheld recorder. 'So Ruby, what would you like to talk about today? You've told us about working in the Larcombes' grocery shop during the war, and Jimmy Larcombe being in love with you. And you've told us you were in love with your GI and were having his baby. I'd love to hear more details about Chet and how you began going out. Only when you're ready, though.'

Petra had turned up the sound system and a throaty-voiced woman began to sing. Ashley and Eddie waited until Ruby had poured her tea, adding milk and stirring it carefully. They could see her reaching back into her memories, the sweet-smelling café fading and World War Two in a little Devon seaside town emerging from the fog of the past. 'I'll Be Seeing You' drifted over their heads as she began to reminisce.

Chapter Seven

'Chet came into the shop,' Ruby began. 'It was early December and we were gearing up for another dismal Christmas. The fifth miserable Christmas of the bloomin' war. 'Course, I recognised him straightaway. It was the fella who jumped out of the Jeep in the high street and gave me that bar of Hershey's and a cheeky smacker. I'd recognise him from the energy alone. So solid and healthy. Not worn out and grey like the rest of us in Berecombe. And he was lovely looking too. Like a film star. Not sure he wanted to buy anything, mind.' She chuckled. 'The Yanks had food and stuff galore. They brought it all over with them and could get anything they wanted in the stores they'd built down on the harbour. Just down from here, it was. They didn't go short of nothing. Between you and me and the gatepost, I think he was bored and nosy. Wanted to see inside a proper English shop, he said. Of course, later, he sweet-talked me and said he'd gone and hunted all over town for the beautiful girl with the red hair. I was known for my hair, you see. Fell all the way to the waist it did, although I always had it pinned up neat and tidy when I was working. Well, you didn't want a hair on your slice of ham, did you?

'Chet had a good look around, leaned against the counter looking all cocky, and gave me a pack of chewing gum. Then he was gone. Well, me and Florrie pored over this thing. All minty, it smelled. We didn't know what to do with it! Jimmy came through from the back and explained. Said some GIs had been passing the stuff around in The Old Harbour pub. Well, we had to try it, didn't we? Lordy, it was peculiar. Why they liked it, I could never fathom. Jimmy and Florrie didn't mind it, but I couldn't be bothered. If I wanted something sweet I'd rather have a lardy cake, that's when you could get hold of one.

'A week passed and then Chet came by again. Not that we minded. They had such lovely manners, the GIs. And the uniforms! We'd never seen the like. Smart jackets and trousers with a crease you could cut your hand on. He only wanted to ask my father permission to take me to a dance, didn't he? Florrie had to explain I had no dad, and up pops Jimmy, saying he was the next best thing. Grilled Chet about his intentions. I wanted the ground to open up and swallow me whole! He got Chet to promise to get me back home by nine, and if he didn't, it would be the end of it. He'd report him to his commanding officer. *Aw Jimmy*, I remember thinking at the time, *kind of you to look out for me.* I didn't know he was sweet on me. Not a clue. He'd never said anything. He didn't say much at all after he'd got out of hospital. Gone into himself, poor lad.

'So I borrowed one of Florrie's frocks. Had to take it in, as I was smaller, and I used the last bit of her red carmine, curled my hair and got collected by Chet. There was another soldier in the Jeep and Iris from the post office. I didn't know her that well. She was one of the local kids who used to throw stones at us evacuees, but she was all right. When I got in the back she whispered, "Stick together and then they can't try any funny business." We held hands and giggled. We were that excited.'

Ruby paused and drank some tea, smiling at the memory. Putting the cup onto its saucer, she continued.

'The dance was in the town hall and we was stopped and checked before we went in. The guards had guns. Imagine! I know it was war, but it was the first time I'd come across a real live gun. The Home Guard didn't have any for years. They ended up using broom handles. Fat lot of good they would have been if Hitler invaded.

'Ooh, it was all so lovely, that dance. My first proper one. There was a real band, made up of GIs. Ever so swish they were, and all along one side there was tables groaning with food. I'd never seen so much food in my life. No booze though. Chet said it was banned and, anyway, none of them drank all that much. The officers didn't want to encourage anything improper, he said. I saw one or two hip flasks coming out on the sly and smelled whisky on their breath though, so some of them drank a bit.

'We danced, although Iris and I weren't nearly as good as some. You should have seen the jitterbugging that went on! Through the legs, up in the air. Petticoats flying. All sorts. We stuck to a nice quickstep or a foxtrot. And then we went for something to eat. I ate a doughnut for the first time, and had salami, although I wasn't so keen on that. And we drank ginger beer and lemonade with ice-cubes, can you imagine? I think it was the most magical night of my life.

'But then Chet had to get me home. I could have stayed and danced all night. Iris and her fella did, so Chet drove me back to the shop; just the two of us. We stopped on the way and had a little kiss; only on the cheek, mind.' Ruby giggled coquettishly. 'Well, all right then, we had a kiss on the lips too. Chet was the perfect gent, though, and I wasn't that sort of girl, I'll have you know. At least not then. My first kiss. I'll never forget it.

'Then he walked me to the side door, bang on nine. I could see the light was on in the back room, so I knew Jimmy and Florrie was still up. They would have got into trouble if the warden had seen that. "Put that light out!" he'd yell. I wasn't thinking about no ARP warden, though. I'd had such a smashing time. Think I floated through that door!'

Chapter Eight

Biddy exploded into the café, bringing in the salty sea-scented air.

'Has it been a good session?' she boomed. 'Are you finished for today? Only I promised I'd take Ruby out to lunch at the new seafood place that's opened in Charmouth. They're doing a pensioner special. We fancy ourselves a bit of lobster, don't we Ruby? We're picking Beryl up on the way, so we need to get going.'

Ashley forced herself back into the vanilla-scented, bustling café. Was it that time already? She was still in 1943 with Chet and a young and excited Ruby at her very first dance. The story had been told so vividly that Ashley could see the dancers and their flushed faces, hear the band and smell the American food that Ruby had found so exotic. She was desperate to know Florrie and Jimmy's reactions to Ruby's relationship with Chet; it was clear Jimmy was very much in love with Ruby already. She felt sorry for him. Back from a long spell in hospital after suffering terribly at Dunkirk, scarred physically and emotionally, and now suffering from unrequited love. She knew only too well how a crushing blow to self-confidence affected how you operated in the world. And, on top of that, Jimmy was trying to cope with what must have been post-traumatic stress disorder. And cope alone. He must have felt he had no chance against Chet, the Hollywood-handsome dashing GI. Her heart went out to him, having to hide his poor scarred face in the back room, keeping away from people's curiosity and well-meaning questions. She had some understanding of how that felt too.

'I think we're done here,' Eddie answered, on her behalf. 'That was some story, Ruby. Have to say it's fascinating to hear how my countrymen were seen when they came over to Berecombe. Golden gods holding the horn of plenty.'

'Well, something like that,' Ruby said crushingly. 'They were certainly glam. Glad to help, dearie,' she added as Ashley helped her with her coat. 'Think I've earned my lobster, and I might even treat myself to a bit of hollandaise to go with it.' She checked a necklace at her throat and tucked the silver locket back under her cardigan. 'Still there,' she muttered.

As soon as she was steady on her feet, Biddy took her arm and they headed towards the prom.

Ashley began to tidy her things away into her rucksack as if to go.

Eddie stayed her arm. 'It would be good if we could talk,' he said hesitantly. 'We've got some air to clear.'

'Is Bree still having your baby?' Ashley bit out without thinking. Oh, why couldn't she shake off this horrible searing jealousy? She was desperate to talk things through with him, but something deep within her stopped the right words coming out. No matter how hard she tried, she couldn't talk to Eddie as she used to. Her whole being wished she could, but Bree and the baby loomed too large. In her mind it was an insurmountable obstacle.

'Ashley, don't go, please. I get that you don't want a relationship with me, but you said we could try to be friends, at least.'

She stood in front of him, hesitating. The café was busy and a group squeezed past her to bag a table. Part of her wanted to flee, the other part just wanted. Tears prickled. This was ridiculous. Why couldn't she and Eddie have something simple like Chet and Ruby? Slumping back into her chair reluctantly, she remembered, to her shame, there had been nothing simple about the situation Chet and Ruby had found themselves in. She recollected the heartfelt letter Ruby had sent her. Young, unmarried and with a baby on the way. It all came back to babies, didn't it? Biting her lip hard, she forced herself out of the self-pitying mood that threatened. 'I don't need to be at the Arts Workshop until later,' she admitted. 'I'm on an afternoon shift there.'

'I could walk you there, if that's okay? It's a nice day. Could do with stretching my legs.'

The thought of walking along in the sunshine with Eddie was almost too much of a temptation. Being close. Smelling his intoxicating hot sandalwood skin. No, she couldn't let it happen. 'I've got a bicycle now. That's what I use to get around town.'

His reaction wasn't what she anticipated. 'Hey, that's great! Gives you some independence. Is it helping you heal?'

'Think so.' Ashley relaxed slightly. 'I was wobbly at first, but I practised and it's coming back to me. You know what they say. Like riding a bike.' It was the weakest attempt at humour, but she could feel herself gradually, treacherously, thawing towards him.

'Great exercise too.'

'It is, but I haven't had the courage to tackle the hill

out of town yet. I'm sticking strictly to the route from the flat to the Arts Workshop and along the seafront.'

'Sounds sensible.'

There was an uncomfortable pause. Had it come to this? Was this all they could manage – a stilted conversation about bicycles? Ashley felt the tears return to thicken her throat. Again, wallowing in the nostalgia that Ruby's memories had evoked, she longed for the simplicity and innocence of a GI dance, with ginger beer and doughnuts, the latest dance craze and chaste first kisses. But Chet had been about to go to war and die, leaving Ruby, his (now not so innocent, pregnant) girl, behind. Theirs had been a relationship made precarious by uncertainty. When staring death in the face, or the possibility of losing the man you've come to passionately love, it was no wonder they'd snatched at any chance of happiness, however fleeting. The situation with Eddie was nothing in comparison.

Stiffening her resolve, she decided that, as there was no way of avoiding Eddie, since Ruby insisted he was present, she needed to overcome this awkwardness. Otherwise she was going to implode. 'Maybe we could have lunch here?' she suggested, half hoping he'd decline. 'I haven't eaten yet.'

Eddie's shoulders visibly dropped. 'I thought you'd

never ask. I'd kill for one of Petra's paninis. Got a craving for a tuna melt.'

Ashley couldn't help but smile. She loved the way he said *toona*. 'You can take the boy out of the US—'

'But I guess you can't take the US out of the boy.'

He turned round to catch Petra's attention, affording Ashley a view of the back of his neck. It was a curiously vulnerable sight and she had to harden her heart against the feelings which overwhelmed her. It was just as well the café was crowded. It stopped her reaching out and throwing her arms around him, burying her face into his neck and kissing him until they were both breathless.

Chapter Nine

Things eased a little between them once they started eating. It was easier to be around Eddie with a plate of food acting as a diversion.

'Will you be going to the D-Day commemoration service?' she asked, tucking into her salad.

'Guess I should. That's if I can get the time free. Term's finished but I've got stuff to tie up. It's on the actual date, isn't it?'

'Yes, on the day of D-Day itself. The sixth of June.'

'What's going to happen?'

Ashley breathed a little more freely. At least if they were talking facts and not emotion, it might be easier. 'There's a service at dawn. It's going to be held on the clifftop where they're also lighting a beacon. From what I can gather, the men all left Berecombe on the morning of the fifth to get to Weymouth and then travelled on to France, arriving in the early hours. Hence the dawn start. I think there'll be prayers and a speech too. The veterans are invited, of course. There's an easy access car park not too far away, otherwise it's a bit of a hike up the cliff path.'

'That's good. I'm sure they'll want to be there.'

'Then there's a church service later in the day and a parade led by the GIs, with the Sea Cadets, a local infantry brigade and anybody else who wants to join in. They're also going to unveil a plaque at some point. Claude, who runs The Old Harbour, is finishing the day in a slightly more informal way with a barbecue, with hot dogs and burgers.'

'Packed day,' Eddie said. 'I'll try to get to as much of it as I can, but I'll definitely attend the early morning service. Sounds as if it's going to be very poignant.'

'I think the names of all the soldiers who went from Berecombe and who died at Omaha are going to be read out too.'

'Then it really will be poignant.'

'I think it will. Let's hope the weather's kind. Oh, and Noah has put together an exhibition of all the archive material from the war. It'll be on special display in the museum until the autumn.'

Eddie laughed. 'Your cousin never stops, does he?'

'He certainly likes to be busy,' Ashley agreed.

'And what about you, Ash? Are you keeping busy too?' Having finished his sandwich, he wiped his hands on a bright pink serviette.

'I've got my work at the Arts Workshop, I'm still taking photographs, and of course there are Ruby's recordings. I'm beginning to go through them, seeing what we can edit, although I don't think Noah will want much missed out, and her memories are getting really exciting now that she's recalling the time when she's older.'

Ashley was glad Eddie had finished eating; the way his lips moved as he tore into his panini had done unspeakable things to her insides. She pushed her plate away, unable to eat any more. She might be having difficulty discussing anything important with him, but there was no denying the reactions of her body. Damping down the raging need, she tried to control herself.

'That dance was something else, wasn't it? I could see it all so vividly.'

She sucked in a breath and concentrated. 'Me too. The food must have been amazing to a girl who'd been on rations for three years. And I love how she didn't know what to do with chewing gum.'

'Guess we were responsible for quite a few things,' Eddie admitted wryly.

'They must have seemed so exotic, these American soldiers. Just as if they'd stepped out of the movies.'

'And yet, really, they were just young boys from Arkansas or Kansas, or the east coast, like me. Ordinary boys thrown into something they had no understanding of, and from which there was every chance they wouldn't get out.'

Ashley sobered, all lustful thoughts fleeing. 'I know the death rate of the men who were billeted in Berecombe was something dreadful. Your grandfather was lucky to survive.'

'That he was. Omaha was a tough place to be. They say there were approximately two thousand casualties amongst the US troops on Omaha alone, but it's impossible to know exactly. Some men were swept out to sea and drowned. It was horror and confusion.'

'Poor Chet.' She shivered, dwelling on his loss. 'I like to think he would have returned to Ruby, had he lived. Married, brought up their children, maybe even made a life here in Berecombe.'

'Speaking of which, you're making quite a life here. Do you think you'll stay?'

Ashley stiffened. The conversation had veered to the personal again. 'I might,' she said vaguely. 'It's too early to tell. Lots of things to be sorted out first. I can't keep living off Noah, so if I do stay, I'll need somewhere permanent to live. But I'm considering it.' She gestured to outside and the inviting breadth of beach and sea. 'What's not to like? And what about you?'

'Me? I'm keeping busy too.'

'It wasn't quite what I meant.' Oops. Why had she let that slip?

'What *did* you mean then, Ashley?'

'Well,' she began, floundering slightly, 'with the baby and everything, I wondered how long you'd stay in England.'

'I can't say it's going to be easy trying to raise a baby when the child is in another country,' he said slowly. 'But, apart from that, there's not a whole heap of stuff that makes me want to go back to the US just yet. In fact, I'm in talks with a production company about making a series of TV programmes. It would be incredibly exciting if I got that off the ground, and it's going to keep me in this part of the world for a while longer, even if they don't renew my lecturing contract at the university.'

Ashley was impressed. She looked at his tanned, open face and at the gentle humour in his soft eyes. 'I think you'd be a hit on television,' she said. So, not only would she have to share him with Bree and the baby, she would also lose him to a television audience of millions.

Shoving down the ungracious thought and wondering where the usual calm, generous Ashley had gone, she pleated a paper serviette between her fingers and listened to Eddie as he talked.

It turned out that Fizz TV was planning to make a series of light-hearted, humorous programmes about British folklore with Harri Morgan and Julia Cooper, a husband-and-wife team. Eddie was to provide on-camera snippets on the historical background.

'It's something I'm really interested in,' he explained. 'Every myth or piece of folklore has a historical basis or reason it came into being. Ash, I'm more excited about this than anything I've done for a while. We're having a major meeting soon and, if that goes well, we'll put out a pilot and see how things go from there. I've met Harri already and think I could work with him.'

The name rang a bell. Then Ashley remembered. Harri Morgan, children's TV presenter, and Julia Cooper, the actress, had been in *Who Dares Dances*, the reality challenge show, a few years before. She recalled the Year Nine girls at school getting very giggly over Harri's Welsh good looks. She smiled at Eddie, pleased for him, but all the while sensing he was inching away from her; moving on to different things which would certainly take him away from Berecombe.

Lunch finished, Eddie walked her out to where her

bicycle was chained up. He admired the bright blue paint job with the little white daisies and – almost – successfully hid his amusement. Thankfully, he didn't hang around to see her wobble along the prom towards the Arts Workshop and Ashley didn't brave turning around to see where he'd gone.

Chapter Ten

As she cycled to work, she congratulated herself on having a reasonably civilised conversation with Eddie and tried hard not to dwell on how good he looked in his jeans and pale blue sweatshirt. It was ironic that, now he was out of bounds, he'd never looked more attractive. Would this longing for him ever go away? Would she ever get over wondering what might have been between them? She pedalled harder, trying to dispel the sexual frustration.

As she entered The Workshop the pong of emulsion paint hit her. She wandered through to the main exhibition area where Ken was supervising a team of volunteers painting the walls and floor white in preparation for Jake's exhibition.

'Hello, my friend,' Ken said as he came over to her. 'Looking good, ain't it?'

Ashley agreed. As a blank backdrop to Jake's stunning paintings, it would be perfect, so she said so. 'Can I ask you a favour?' she added.

'Steam ahead.'

'Would it be possible for me to hold Ruby's living memories sessions here? The café is getting busy now the tourist season is underway and it's quite noisy. We're getting some good stuff from Ruby and I want every word to be heard.'

'Can't see that being a problem. You could use the staff room or one of the tutorial spaces. Staff room is cosy, though, and has closer proximity to the kettle.'

Ashley went with her impulse and threw her arms around him. 'Thanks, Ken, that would be great.'

'Get off me, you daft mare,' he said good-naturedly. 'Will the man mountain that is Eddie be joining you?'

Ashley pulled a face. 'For some reason Ruby wants him there. Knowing my luck, Biddy will probably want to join in as well. It could get a bit crowded.'

Ken laughed. 'Now there's a life you want recorded. I reckon you could mount an exhibition of that life on its own. Might need to be X-rated, though.'

'Is it true she ran a brothel in London?'

Ken winced. 'Don't ever let her hear you call it that,'

he said. 'My understanding is, it was a very high-class affair. Think she's known to a whole generation of MPs and senior CEOs. She's a wonderful woman, is Biddy. If you want to pull any strings, she's the one. Think she can blackmail half the male population over a certain age in London. Not to mention Devon. Quite a girl.'

'Maybe we could call in some favours on behalf of Jake, then?'

'What makes you think I haven't already?' Ken chuckled. 'Speaking of which, here's the man of the moment now.'

As Jake came into the room, he seemed to fill it, so charismatic was his presence. There was something special about him. He had a celebrity-like aura that was intoxicating. Ashley remembered reading a biography of Picasso and how people commented on his animal magnetism, his sheer power and genius. She had a taste of that, now, looking at Jake.

He stood for a second, admiring the work that was going on. 'Looking good in here,' he said. 'Hi, Ashley.' He turned to her, staring intently. 'You know, I was serious about you sitting for me. I'd really love to add your portrait to the exhibition.'

Ashley felt herself blush. 'I really don't think I've got the time.'

'Aw, go on with you. I've got nothing for you to do

this afternoon that won't wait,' Ken put in. 'Studio One's free. Help yourself, my lovelies.'

Ashley hesitated. She wasn't sure she wanted to be painted, especially by an artist like Jake. She suspected he missed nothing.

'Please, Ashley,' he begged.

'Go on, my friend,' Ken stirred, enjoying her discomfort. 'You'll end up with a portrait to hang on your wall. Think what a talking point that will be and, if nothing else, it will give a starving painter some life-drawing practice. You wouldn't deny an artist that, surely?'

Ashley gave him daggers, then relented. At least all she had to do was sit and stare into space; it might give her some thinking room. And besides, she had to admit her ego was flattered by the thought that someone wanted to paint her. She was curious to see what bits of her personality would end up on the canvas. She followed Jake into the main studio.

They set themselves up directly underneath the roof windows. Jake sat her so that she was half-facing away from him. She made sure her hair fell over her face, thankfully hiding the side with the scar. Away from all the activity in the exhibition space, the air hung heavy and intimate.

'I'd like to start with some sketches, if that's okay?' he asked. 'What am I saying? You're an artist, so you know the score.'

'I'm hardly an artist,' she answered. 'I taught art, but that's a very different thing.' As she spoke, she was aware of Jake's pencil making rapid marks on the paper he'd pinned on an easel.

'Not what Ken says,' Jake grunted, hampered by the 4B he held between his teeth. 'He said the stuff he'd seen of yours is really great.'

'That's kind of him. I may have a certain talent for water-colours, but I'm nowhere near your league.'

Jake concentrated on the marks he was making, frowning as he did so, and then he stopped. 'Don't think it's something Ken is just being kind about. When it comes to art, he tells the absolute truth. It's one thing I really admire about him.'

'I'm happy to take the compliment, then.' *And forgive him for pushing me into this,* she added silently. Deflecting the conversation away from herself, she said, 'Are you excited about the exhibition?'

'You bet. Looking forward to having the paintings back from the framers. They've gone to the place Ken's son works at. Makes them look completely different once they're in a frame, but it's not something I can afford to do very often. Mostly I just leave them on the raw canvas.'

'Depends on the painting, I suppose. I quite like how some of the ones on the unframed canvas look. Seems to suit your style somehow.' Ashley shifted to get more comfortable. The sunlight, streaming in through the ceiling windows, was very warm. It was relaxing her. 'What are you hoping comes from it? The exhibition, I mean.'

Jake blew out a breath. 'It would be good to get stuff in a London gallery, I suppose. Get some exposure. At the moment, all I do is paint hard and not get anywhere. I'd like to be offered a commission for a high-profile portrait, maybe something corporate.'

He was ambitious, Ashley observed. 'As long as they're not bored rich women who want to make a move on you?'

He grinned, taking the pencil from his mouth. 'Yeah, as long as I can avoid that.'

'Well, I promise I won't make a move on you.' She turned her head slightly so that she could better check his expression.

'Well, you see, if you were to make a move, I might not object too much.' He put all his pencils down, propelled the chair on its wheels out from behind the easel and stared at her, unabashed.

Ashley suppressed a giggle. Hiding behind her hair, she reflected that Jake must be at least five years younger than her, but he had the confidence of someone much more experienced. For a second, she felt a glimmer of sympathy for the bored London ladies. She wondered who had actually seduced whom.

Chapter Eleven

At zero four hundred hours on the morning of June the sixth Ashley and Noah made their way, in the grey half-light, up the path from the car park to the clifftop where the D-Day commemoration service was due to be held. They didn't speak. Maybe it was the brutally early hour or perhaps it was the poignancy of the occasion. One or two others stumbled along the path behind them, and Noah went to the aid of a middle-aged woman pushing Victor in his wheelchair. Ashley accompanied them, walking stick in hand, concentrating on not tripping; she was only half awake. Their breath misted in the still cool pre-dawn and there was expectation in the air, along with the promised warmth of the day.

Once at the top, Ashley went to stand behind Biddy

and Arthur. Biddy turned and nodded a welcome. Three other veterans had made the climb and found their place with Erica, the vicar who was leading the service, who was standing by the unlit beacon. In the east, a glimmer of pink crowned the horizon and cast a glow on the faces of those present. It was very still, very sombre. All that could be heard was the shush of the sea far below and the keening of a solitary gull. Ashley found herself holding her breath, the beginning of tears clenching in her throat. A few more people joined the group, and she was aware of a tall, solid presence beside her.

'This is going to be quite something,' Eddie whispered in her ear. He reached for her hand and she let him take it.

'Hey, you're shivering!' he exclaimed. 'Come here.' He opened his coat and gently pulled her inside, standing behind and banding his strong arms around her.

'Better?' he asked as he rested his chin on the top of her head.

Ashley tensed. Her brain snapped into flight mode, but her body wanted to stay. Accepting there was nowhere else she'd rather be, she nodded, not trusting her voice. She allowed herself to relax and concentrated on the feel of his heart beating and his breath stirring her hair. The warmth coming off his body was bliss.

The Great Summer Street Party Part 2

The service was sweet and short. Erica said a prayer and gave her thanks to the men who made the ultimate sacrifice. The mayor gave a short speech and then one of the veterans read out, in a voice trembling with age and emotion, the names of those who had died. It was a long list, his voice a mere whisper, and some of the names could barely be heard against a sea breeze that had whipped up. The sun sent great rivulets of pink and orange across the wide sky and, as Erica read out Laurence Binyon's immortal lines, the mayor lit the beacon. The flames shot into the air, joining the blazing sunrise.

The quiet was punctuated only by the fire crackling, people sniffling and the odd murmur of muted conversation. In front of Ashley and Eddie, Arthur blew his nose and Biddy put a hand to his arm as if to reassure him. The touching gesture was almost too much.

The event had been unbearably moving and Ashley was thankful she'd witnessed it, and glad she'd made the effort of the climb up. Eddie, with a whisper of a sigh, released her from his coat and she was hit by a blast of chill wind coming off the sea. Swaying a little, she steadied herself with her stick. It was as if part of herself was gone. She watched as, with his head bowed with emotion, he walked away. She longed to follow. Noah came to stand beside her and took her hand. He remained unusually silent, overcome with emotion from the service.

Biddy turned to them, her over-loud voice splintering the mood. 'Are you two walking back down to the car park?' she asked. 'Petra's putting on a breakfast at the caff. You'll need something hot inside you after standing out here.'

Ashley nodded and she and Noah began to walk with them but, halfway there, she changed her mind. 'I will come for breakfast, but I think I'll just stay here a while longer. Absorb the atmosphere. Maybe take some photographs.'

'Suit yourself,' Biddy boomed. 'Come on then, Arthur, stir your stumps. We need to get back to collect Ruby.'

'Sure you'll be okay?' Noah asked. 'I'm not keen on leaving you up here. The going's quite rough, Ash.'

'I'll be fine. A bit stiff from standing, but I'll ease up when I get moving. And at least it's light enough to see properly now. You go back with Biddy and Arthur. I'm sure there'll be someone around to give me a lift. Or I can get a bus.' She watched as he followed the rest of the group down the slope and through the gate to the car park, and then she was left alone. Or so she thought. A tall bulky figure detached itself from the shadowy trees.

'Mind if I keep you company?' Eddie asked. 'I'll go if

you'd rather be alone.' He gestured to somewhere vague behind him. 'I had to get away for a moment. It was too much.'

Of course. His grandfather had fought at Omaha, probably alongside some of the men who had died and whom they had honoured today. She was touched by his sensitivity. She smiled at him. What could it hurt? They turned uphill and walked the short distance back to the burning beacon. The warmth it gave off was fierce and welcome and, with the chilly air now being chased off by the heat of the June morning, it felt sunny and peaceful.

Ashley scanned the coast, from Portland slumbering in the east, across the flat sea to the hints of Berry Head in the west. The breeze returned and a gull lifted and flew, dipping over the water, calling its mournful cry. They didn't speak, there seemed no need for words, but Eddie put an arm around her shoulders, hugging her close, and she didn't resist. A new understanding flowed between them, confused and uncertain, tentative and wordless but profound. All was silence bar the crash of the waves and the hiss and crackle of the burning beacon. Ashley was sure the clamour of her heart drowned everything out.

The gull shot across in front of them, cackling. It broke them apart. She moved a little nearer to the beacon and away from Eddie. She held out her hands to warm them, but it was simply an excuse to give her time to think; to put her churning emotions into some kind of coherent order. It was torture being close to him when she couldn't have him. Not as she wanted. She'd offered him friendship but she could see no way through this craving for him, this primal need in her gut, in order to discover that friendship. Tears threatened again but this time they were for her and for what she refused to let herself have.

The moment hung hard and heavy but neither spoke. Ashley tried to form the words and sensed Eddie was waiting patiently, but none came.

'Coffee?' he asked eventually, admitting defeat as the moment for talking had soared away with the breeze and drifted over the sea. 'I've got my car with me. I can give you a lift.'

'Perfect.'

The conversation was mundane, between two mere acquaintances; it was profoundly depressing. All intimacy between them had fled. They were back to square one.

Chapter Twelve

Petra had opened up especially for them and had set up a big table on one side of the café. Erica and the mayor, Biddy and Arthur, now joined by Ruby, were already tucking into bacon and eggs. Apart from a few others who had been at the service, the café was empty.

'Sit yourselves down, you two; two full English?' Petra asked, pad in hand.

They nodded and sat next to Ruby on the end. The warmth of the café, with its everyday fug of sizzling bacon, was a welcome contrast to the clifftop service.

'Noah not here?' Ashley said, summoning a smile for the old woman, who was dressed in a pure white twinset today.

'He's gone to give some interview or other to a

woman from the local rag. She couldn't get to the service herself, so he's gone to fill her in, he said.'

'Good luck to him.' Ashley pulled a face. 'I think Keeley's got the hots for him. You didn't feel up to it either, Ruby?'

'No, dearie. When you get to my age you've had your fill of remembrance services. I'll maybe go to church later, with Biddy and Arthur. More my style.'

'And much easier to get to,' Ashley added as she took the mug of coffee from Petra and clutched it to her, welcoming its warmth. 'It was quite a tricky walk up in the dark.'

'How was it then?'

'Very moving. I expected it to be poignant, but not as much as it actually was. Hard to hold the tears back.'

Ruby nodded sadly, 'Too many men gone.'

'All their names were read out.'

'Including Chet's, I expect.'

'Do you know, I didn't hear his. Poor Victor was getting worn out by then and it was difficult to hear what he was saying. The wind had got up too and his voice was carried out to sea. Where are the veterans, anyway?'

'Back in their hotel, I expect. With a drop of the good stuff in their coffee.'

Ashley smiled. 'I wouldn't blame them. It was

surprisingly cold up there until the sun came up properly, but I'm glad I went.' Petra put down two plates groaning with eggs and bacon, and Ashley concentrated on eating, suddenly ravenous. When she'd got to the second coffee stage, she sat back, replete. 'So good.'

'I like your breakfasts over here,' Eddie said, speaking for the first time since they'd entered the café; he'd been withdrawn and silent up to now. 'But you can't beat a bit of bacon and maple syrup.' He scraped some marmalade onto the last piece of toast and ate it.

'Maple syrup,' Ruby said wistfully. 'Chet told me he had it on his pancakes. There's a place in Blackheath, near home, near where I live in London. Proper American diner. Must get Serena to take me, if the woman ever gets a second free. They do pancakes and maple syrup.'

'Sounds good, ma'am.'

Eddie's voice was so melancholy, Ashley wondered if he was thinking of his home. He must miss it. Or maybe he was thinking about Bree and the baby? She had no idea if the woman was still in England.

'So is Chet the one who used to call Florrie "Ma'am"?' he asked.

'He was. Used to make us all chuckle.' Ruby's eyes narrowed as she remembered. 'So polite, those boys.

After he'd taken me to the dance, he used to pop in regular. First time he came in, I was singing my head off and didn't see him. I was that embarrassed! Then he started coming for a cuppa up in the parlour with me and Florrie. Said he loved English tea. Can you imagine? Used to bring us stuff like tinned ham, chocolate and nylons. Ooh, those nylons were smashing. You had to be careful, though. Lots of girls were turning tricks for less. You had to be careful about your reputation. You didn't want to be getting a name.' She turned to Ashley. 'You got your recorder thingy with you?'

Ashley nodded, surprised Ruby was in the mood for more memories. She reached around to fish it out of her rucksack. As she slid it onto the table and switched it to record, Eddie asked Ruby a question.

'Do you remember when they left for Omaha? Left Berecombe, I mean.'

It seemed as if his thoughts still lay with the men whose lives they had just commemorated.

'I do. As a matter of fact, I was just thinking of it. Seventy-five years ago, but I remember it like yesterday. Iris ran down the hill from the post office, all breathless. Hammered on the side door. Said she'd heard from Vera, who ran the bed and breakfast where some of the officers were staying, that the balloon was up. They was shipping out.'

'Did you know anything about what they were going into?'

Ruby eyed him shrewdly. 'Well, we knew they weren't over here for the good of their health. They'd spent the time training. Manoeuvres on the beach, crawling under barbed wire and all sorts. Chet told me a bit about it. That's when they weren't playing baseball up at the camp on the hill. Iris and me went to watch a game one time. We thought it would be ever so exciting. Didn't know what to expect. Turns out it's rounders.'

She was so indignant, Eddie smiled.

'We knew they were off to France. That there was a big push of some kind. But it didn't do to talk.' She tapped the side of her nose. 'Careless talk and all that. Chet didn't tell me anything much, but I knew he was scared and I knew he thought he might not get through. We just made the most of the time we had together. We knew it was going to end. Lived in the moment. Didn't talk about the past and certainly not the future, when we feared there wouldn't be one.'

Addressing Ashley, she said, 'I told you about those two little girls dying, didn't I? One minute innocently playing Pooh sticks on the bridge, and the next... Focuses your mind on the here and now, hearing about something like that happening, no question. Always waiting to see if a bomb had your name on it. Makes everything sharp and vivid. Makes what little life you've got all the sweeter.

'Chet didn't talk about the army much, but he told me about life at home, about maple syrup on his pancakes, about his ma and pa, about the lobster he used to eat on the beach at home. Think that's why he liked Berecombe; it reminded him of where he came from.' She wrinkled her nose. 'He told me his proper name once but it was a funny one, foreign, and I couldn't get my teeth round it.' She shrugged thin shoulders. 'Everyone called him Chet, so Chet was good enough for me.'

'What happened on the morning they shipped out?' Eddie stirred his coffee thoughtfully.

'Well, like I said, Iris comes knocking at the door and we went to stand on the high street. There was quite a crowd gathered by that time, even though it was sparrow's fart. The boys had been part of the town for six months and we'd welcomed them in and, mostly, they'd behaved and not caused any bother. The town wanted to say goodbye to them. Wanted to say thank you and *bon voyage*. Wanted to wish them good luck. There were a few tears in the crowd, I can tell you, and more than one war bride. Stella Young had made quick work of it. Got her soldier to marry her by April.'

'Did he come back?' Ashley asked. 'Her husband?'

Ruby shook her head. 'Drowned, she heard. Didn't stand a chance, some of them. The story that got back to us was the water was too deep when they got off them landing craft things. A lot of them sank under the weight of their kit. Poor lad, he was only twenty.' She fell silent and Ashley reached for her hand.

'Those boys marching off,' Ruby continued in a wavering voice. 'I remember it so vividly. We heard them coming, marching down the hill, boots thumping, all rhythmic, in formation, like. Iris and I went mad. Me screaming Chet's name and her Glenn's, her sweetheart. We caught a glimpse of them, tight faces, helmets covered in camouflage and their kit on their bellies. Don't think they saw us, although I swear Chet looked round. Some of them was throwing stuff into the crowd. Chocolate and gum, sweets for the kiddies. And money. They were throwing their English money away! I asked Ernie Small the butcher about it. He'd been in the first show and had come back a bit doolally in the head, but he knew about war. Do you know what he said?'

'What?' Ashley whispered.

Ruby bent nearer. 'They was throwing their money away because they knew they wouldn't need it again.'

Ashley sucked in a breath. 'You mean—'

'They knew the chance of survival was low,' Eddie

said. 'Jeez. Imagine knowing that where you might be going, you'd have no use for money of any kind.'

All three remained silent for a moment.

Ruby's mouth worked as she struggled to find the words to continue. 'And that's the last I saw of Chet. Didn't know he'd left me a souvenir, did I?' She pushed her teacup away. 'Later we found out they'd gone to Weymouth. Place was heaving, we heard. Troops from all over had congregated and were queuing up, waiting for the off. Iris' cousin said she had them blocking the road outside her house for hours. She let them use her garage to brew up some coffee. When they finally shifted off, she found they'd left a big sack of the stuff as a thank you. Proper ground coffee, it was. Well, she was used to Camp, wasn't she? We hadn't seen real coffee since 1940. She boiled some of it up and spat it out. Didn't like it! Gave it away, she did. They'd scratched their names on her wall too. As a memento. Wonder how many of *them* got through?'

'They estimate over four thousand Allied troops died that day,' Eddie said in a low voice. 'So probably not many of those soldiers survived. I guess the men were leaving their mark. Show they were there.'

'Well, that's as may be. Me and Iris went up to the camp to have a look-see afterwards. Place was deserted. Stuff lying all round. I picked up a leather glove. I kept it for months, fancying it was one of Chet's. Used to cry myself to sleep over it, thinking his hands would be cold without his gloves. Daft bugger, I was. As if cold hands were what he'd be worried about. On one of the tents was painted, in big red letters, "So long, Berecombe." We knew they'd really gone then. It hit us. Hit us hard. Iris cried like a baby. The following morning, we were all woken up early on again, but this time it was planes going overhead. Hundreds and hundreds of them. Went on for hours. In the end, me and Iris went down to the beach and watched them go over. We couldn't sleep, it was too noisy. Huddled together on a bench watching them roar over our heads out to France. We knew something big was happening then. They didn't stop even when the sun came up.

'The town was ever so funny afterwards. Like a ghost town. One minute they'd filled it, the next they'd gone, as if they'd never been there. They'd brought all this colour and life, you see, all this bustle and excitement, not to mention the chocolate, the ciggies and the sweeties. You'll call it candy, won't you, young Eddie?'

Eddie nodded.

'Then all of a sudden, the place was deserted, empty. It was so quiet. And boring. No dances to look forward to, no smart chap on your arm to take you to the pictures. Then I found out I was having a kiddie and there were ructions then, I can tell you.' She leaned back, exhausted from talking. 'But that'll save for another day.' She eyed them beadily. 'Won't it?'

'We'll save that for another day, Ruby,' Ashley said kindly and clicked off the recorder.

Chapter Thirteen

'Just turn to the light slightly. That's it. Perfect. Don't move.'

Ashley and Jake were in Studio One again. It was the first proper sitting for her portrait. After taking numerous photos on his phone and drawing dozens of preliminary sketches, Jake had asked her to sit for him so he could begin painting. Once she'd overcome her initial embarrassment, she found it a soothing process. Now he was painting, he talked less. She had the feeling he drifted off into some kind of alternative mind-set. As long as she took regular breaks, she was actually enjoying being forced to sit and do nothing. The one downside was she had plenty of time to dwell on Eddie.

He hadn't stayed long after Ruby's impromptu session in the café. With a preoccupied expression, he'd said his goodbyes and had gone. Ashley wondered if he'd been disturbed by Ruby's recollections of the suffering at D-Day. After all, as well as Chet, it had involved his grandfather, too. She wanted to ask Noah for Eddie's number but hardened her heart. He probably still had Bree around to console him. The temptation to fall into bitterness was seductive. And yet, Ruby's words about Chet lodged in her thoughts. Ruby must have known her time with Chet was limited and that it was unlikely she'd ever see him again after the war, yet she embraced the experience. Lived in the moment. No introspection. No regrets. Was there a lesson for her there? Was she so wrapped up with the spectre of Eddie's ex and the forthcoming baby that she was going to let it jeopardise any future relationship she could have with him? Maybe she should also try living in the moment?

When their little group left the café, Ashley, unable to face the church service, wandered to where the plaque was going to be unveiled in the remembrance square. The ceremony was going to be the finale of the parade. The Stars and Stripes, the Union flag and the distinctive green, white and black flag of Devon fluttered in the breeze, but the plaque itself was hidden under a cloth. After checking no one was around, she lifted it and took some photographs.

> *Dedicated to the brave soldiers who made the supreme sacrifice, and to those who fell injured, to save us from the yoke of evil and ensure the freedom and liberty of Europe. It is also dedicated to the people of Berecombe who welcomed men far from home into their own homes and community. The bond between the soldiers of the US Army and the citizens of this town will never be broken.*

Tears again threatened. Damn, what was it about today that nailed the emotions to the surface? She found a seat in the sun and waited until the parade, led by the five remaining GIs, with the Rifles Brigade, Sea Cadets and various dignitaries following on, had arrived. Noah walked with the mayor and other councillors and looked taut and serious. It was the culmination of this part of the year's commemorations and certainly the most important. From her tucked-away position, she took photographs using the telephoto lens, so as not to be intrusive.

Eddie hadn't attended the plaque unveiling and now it was Saturday, and the next Ruby session was due to take place here at the Arts Workshop. She shifted slightly. She wished it was easier being around him.

'Ashley, I said, do you want to take a break? Comfort break, get a coffee?' Jake's voice broke into her thoughts. 'You were miles away. You okay, maid?'

'Sorry, Jake. Got lost in my mind.' She stretched and winced at how stiff she felt. 'How long have we been at this session?'

'My bad.' He glanced at the clock on the wall. 'Sheesh. Two hours straight. Once I get into the zone, I lose all track of time.'

'Can I have a look?'

'No,' he snapped, throwing a cloth over the canvas. 'Sorry. Rather you didn't. Not until it's finished.' He slid her a look from under thick dark lashes. 'I'm a bit neurotic about my work until it's done. And even then I've been known to scrap it if I'm not happy.'

'No problem. Let's grab that coffee then, shall we?' Ashley stretched again and eased out her left leg. She cast a curious look at the hidden canvas; she was dying to see it.

The door opened and a slight girl with a heart-shaped face, a shock of pink hair and a nose ring looked in. 'Sorry, guys, I was looking for Ken. Have you seen him?' She held up a basket. 'Brought some lunch goodies down from the café. Shall I put it in the staff room?'

Jake got up. Dropping his brushes in a jar filled with water, he wiped his paint-covered hand on his jeans. 'Here, let me. We were heading that way for a coffee anyway.'

'Oh, thanks, man. That thing is heavier than a very heavy thing.' She handed it over. 'I'm Zoe. You must be the new *wunderkind*.'

They shook hands and he smiled, cocking his head on one side flirtatiously. 'Jake Tremayne.' Turning, he introduced Ashley.

Zoe's jaw dropped. 'So, you're Ashley? I've heard loads about you from Granddad and Biddy.'

'Hi there. You must be Arthur's granddaughter. The one who's at university?'

'That's me. Just finished my second year. Durham, for my sins. Home for the break and working in the café.'

'Must make a change from uni.'

'You could say that,' Zoe replied cheerfully. 'But it's always good to come home to Devon.'

'Is that the dulcet tones of a Zoe I hear?' Ken came into the room and threw his arms around her. 'How are you, girl? Still painting or have you permanently gone over to the dark side of English Literature?'

'Hi, Ken,' she said with a laugh. 'Not much time to paint. Not sure I have the talent either.'

'Not another one,' Ken growled. He gathered Zoe and

Ashley up and began to lead them to the staff room. 'What is it with you people? Why do I spend my life forcing you to acknowledge your talents? You staying for lunch, Zoe, my friend?'

'Well, seeing as I lumped it all the way here…'

'Nonsense, child. I saw your mother's old jalopy parked outside. I assume you borrowed it.'

'Busted.' Zoe giggled. 'But yes, I'd love to stay for lunch. I've finished for the day at the caff.'

Ken made coffee while the others found plates and cutlery and shared out the food.

'God, this looks good,' Jake said, cutting up a BLT. 'I'm starving.'

'Well, she's no Millie, but Petra can deal up a mean sandwich,' Zoe said. She ripped open a bag of crisps. 'Try a tuna mayo, I made those. Ken's beloved Tessa made the granary loaf. It's gorge.'

'Then I must.' Jake shot her a look from sapphire-blue eyes that made her blush.

Ashley hid a smile. It would seem flirting was rooted deep in Jake's DNA. She couldn't blame Zoe's reaction; the man's aura was starry.

'You bloomin' eating again, child?' a familiar voice called from the door.

'Busted,' Ashley said, and winked at Zoe. 'Ruby,' she cried. 'Come on in, there's plenty to go around.' She jumped up and grabbed a chair to squeeze in at the table. 'You're early.'

'Is there room for me too?'

It was Eddie.

'Yes.' Ridiculously flustered, Ashley found another chair.

'It's my fault Ruby's early. I gave her a lift.'

'Oh, that's good,' Ashley said lamely. She winced and willed herself to act normally. She couldn't. Everything about Eddie made her prickle.

Ken put a cafetière of coffee on the table. 'No problem, my friend. We'd still be eating this food come Christmas if you hadn't turned up. Mind, I've heard about you, Ruby. You look like a sparrow but can eat your own weight in teacakes.'

Ruby giggled, taking it as the joke it was meant to be. 'Get off with you, young man. You've got to have a few vices when you're my age. It's the only thing that keeps me going.'

'If you're staying with Biddy, I should think she's taught you a thing or two about vices.' He poured the coffee, rich and aromatic, into mugs.

'Oi, lay off my step-granny, you,' Zoe protested. 'She's my favourite old person.'

'She won't be if she hears you calling her that,' Ken responded drily.

Ashley sipped coffee, enjoying the banter. She tried not to look at Eddie, aware he had on some kind of loose olive-green linen shirt that enhanced his suntan. Trying to ignore the longing which heated her face, she put down her sandwich, all appetite gone. Staring at her plate, she could hear him having a conversation with Zoe about her university course. Looking up, she caught Jake's eye; he wore a curious expression and she felt herself blush even more.

Chapter Fourteen

Zoe asked if she could stay to listen in on the memories session.

Ruby readily agreed. 'Be nice to have a young 'un around,' she said. 'I miss my grandchildren,' she added, clutching at Zoe's hand. 'Most are all grown up now, of course, with little ones of their own, so I don't get to see much of them.'

Once their lunch things had been tidied away and Ken and Jake had returned to work, Ashley made a pot of tea and got the handheld recorder out in readiness.

Zoe picked it up and turned it over curiously. 'I've never seen one of these things. It's way cool.' She put it down. 'Why don't you just use your phone though?'

Ashley suddenly felt very old. 'I've no idea,' she

admitted. 'You'll have to ask my cousin, Noah. He's the one who's in charge of all this.'

'And it's going into an exhibition later in the year?'

'Yes. September, I believe.'

'Sweet. I'll still be around then.'

'Well, I might not be if you don't get a move on,' Ruby said with asperity. 'Haven't got all day, Ashley.'

'Sorry, Ruby. I'm all ready now. What would you like to talk about today?' She shot a glance at Eddie who had a careful, neutral sort of expression on his face. 'The aftermath of D-Day?'

The old woman sucked her teeth. 'Not in the mood. What about when Chet and I started walking out? Not as gloomy.'

Zoe clasped her mug of tea to her, eyes glowing. 'Oh, is this your GI? Biddy told me all about him. I'd love to hear more. Bet it was a bit different to a quick fumble in the Undercroft Bar, like I'm used to.'

Ruby raised her eyebrows at the girl. 'Just a bit, I'd say.'

Ashley switched on the recorder.

'What sort of things did you do?' Zoe asked. 'Was there much you could do, I mean, with the war on and everything?'

'We managed,' Ruby answered, folding her hands primly. 'We took walks along the clifftop, over past the

Radar Station, although we couldn't get all that close, of course. There was a good deal of barbed wire.'

'Where was the Radar Station?' Eddie asked.

'Up on Bere Cliffs.'

'Oh, I know it,' Zoe exclaimed. 'Dad told me about it when I was a kid. It's the National Trust hut now. They do teas and ice-creams. And you're right, there are some ace walks up there. You can walk for miles. And get lost in the bracken. Sean and I used to go up there when we wanted to get away from The Olds.' She blushed. 'I used to go out with Sean Tizzard before uni. It's how I know Ken and Tessa.'

Ruby sniffed. 'I suppose we were doing much the same. We'd hide away, do a bit of courting, like.' She sighed. 'There was one place we'd head for. Had views right across the bay. Great big shimmering views as far as the end of the world. We'd keep quiet and watch the rabbits, and even deer. When it was warm, there'd be basking adders up there too. For a girl from London, it was like a different world. And sometimes, when there were no boats in the bay, you could forget there was a war on. Not that that happened very often, unfortunately.'

'Although it was the war that brought you Chet,' Eddie offered.

'That's right, young man.' Ruby peered at Eddie. She

frowned. 'You do remind me of him. Maybe it's the voice. Where are you from?'

'Rockport, Massachusetts, originally, ma'am.'

'Yes, it's the voice. You've got the same sort of Yank accent.'

'Where did Chet come from?'

'I'm not sure I remember rightly. On the coast, not far from Boston, or some such.'

'Same ballpark. It's no wonder we sound alike.'

'He wasn't as tall as you.' Ruby eyed Eddie's shoulders. 'Not as big neither. And, of course, he had on his uniform. Not jeans. How old are you?'

'Coming up to thirty-seven.'

She patted his hand, her eyes misting. 'Such a child.'

Zoe huffed and rolled her eyes.

'I must seem ancient to Zoe here.' He mustered a grin.

'It's not that,' the girl said impatiently. 'I want to hear more about Chet and Ruby. It all sounds so romantic. How old were you, Ruby, when all this was happening?'

'I was sixteen. Only just, mind. Chet was nineteen.'

'You were so young. I don't think Mum would have let *me* date a boy at that age and wander around the Bere Cliffs with him, getting up to all sorts.'

Ruby snorted. 'Doubt if you was much older when you went up there with your Sean. Things were different back then, mind. My generation had to grow up fast.'

'So, where else did he take you?'

'We went to the pictures. There's no picture house here now, I see, but back then there was a smasher at the top of the hill.'

'That's where the Co-op is now,' Zoe said, nodding vigorously. 'Man, I'd literally die for a cinema in Berecombe. It's a right miz going all the way into Exeter.'

'It was difficult to get tickets, especially when the GIs were here. They bought them all up, but Stella Young's mum ran it, so she used to save us a few. There'd be me and Chet and Iris and Glenn and Stella and her husband-to-be. We'd have real larks.'

'What was on? What were the hot films of the day?'

Ruby smiled at Zoe's enthusiasm. 'A Gracie Fields film was always popular. I liked *Shipyard Sally*. We all came out singing "Wish Me Luck As You Wave Me Goodbye".'

'Who's Gracie Fields?'

Ruby laughed. 'Look her up, young lady. There was *Gentleman Jim* with Errol Flynn, he was always a favourite. Oh, and *Mrs Miniver* with Greer Garson. That had us all in tears. *Casablanca*, of course.'

'I've seen *Casablanca*! It's a classic. Did you sit in the back row and snog?'

'Zoe!' Ashley exclaimed.

Ruby cackled. 'No, we did not, young lady. The

usherette used to walk up and down the aisles and have a nosy to check there was no funny business going on.'

Zoe hooted. 'Can you imagine that happening now?'

'I cannot. The last time Serena took me to the pictures it was like a bun fight. Kiddies running everywhere, folks on their phones.'

'What else did you do? Were you going out with him at Christmas? That must have been different when the war was on. No piles of presents, no mountains of food.' Zoe stopped, aghast. 'Did you even *have* Christmas Day?'

'Of course we did, child,' Ruby said, indulging her. 'But it wasn't like it is now.' Ruby's face took on a dreamy look and she began talking so intensely that no one, including Zoe, wanted to interrupt.

'By December 1943 Chet had taken me to the dance and had spent a lot of time in the front parlour of the flat, drinking tea with me and Florrie. I think Florrie was of a mind that if she had us under her roof we couldn't get up to much.' Ruby's lips twisted. 'Considering what happened the next year, she probably had a point. But more than Chet being my beau, Florrie wanted to make the boys feel welcome, knowing they was a long way from home and their own families. Iris and Glenn would come along and it would be quite a party. Jimmy didn't often join us. I thought at the time it was because he was shy about his scar, but I learned better later on.

The Great Summer Street Party Part 2

'Coming up to Christmas, Florrie invited Chet and Glenn to Christmas dinner. Iris, too. Florrie couldn't think of anything worse than not being with your family at Christmas, and I know she hoped that if her Jimmy had ever been in the same situation, another mother would have looked after him in the same way. We saved all our meat rations for weeks so we could put on a half-decent spread. Funny thing was, Chet turned us down, saying he'd be on guard duty that day. I knew something was up, because the men used to take it in turns to do it, and he and Glenn were on not long before. I remember because the weather had turned and they were out in a storm all night.

'So I said to Florrie that something wasn't right, and we took ourselves off to the camp and asked the chap on the gate to check the rota. Turns out Chet and Glenn weren't due on guard duty again until January. The next time they came for tea we asked them. Well, what they said as an answer would make a glass eye weep. Florrie wept buckets. Turns out they knew we didn't have much on ration and they didn't want to have off us what little we had. They were such thoughtful lads; they knew an outright refusal would have offended, so they made up this daft story about being on duty.

'Florrie, when she'd stopped bawling, had no truck with any of this and insisted they come for their

Christmas dinner. Well, on the morning they arrived, they came carrying this enormous parcel. It was one someone had sent them from home. From America! Had two salami sausages in it, chocolate, some of that teaberry chewing gum, cans of brisket and – wonder of wonders – five cans of pineapple! I'd never had pineapple, not even before the war, and I've never forgotten how sweet it tasted.

'We had such a good time. I don't think I've ever eaten so much food and felt so full. We played charades and sang some songs and carols. We had paper chains all across the ceiling made from newspaper, and hats too. We raised a glass to absent friends and family, and that got Florrie tearing up again, and the rest of us weren't far off having a sniffle. Can't say it was the best Christmas Day I've ever had, but it was the most memorable. Even Jimmy joined in, sort of.'

'No presents?' Zoe asked softly.

Ruby chuckled. 'Not what you'd think of as presents. We were lucky if we got a stocking with some nuts and a silver sixpence in my day, war or no war. Florrie gave me a pair of earrings that had belonged to her mother and Jimmy gave me some gloves, which I think he'd got Florrie to knit.'

'What did Chet get you?'

Ruby's eyes misted over. Her hand went to the silver locket around her neck.

'And you've worn it ever since? Oh!' The sound was long and wistful. 'Ruby, it's all so romantic.'

'Maybe, child. Maybe.' She reached over and patted the girl's hand. 'Now, I've sat here long enough and talked myself hoarse. Why don't you show me around this place? I could do with stretching my legs.'

Chapter Fifteen

Ashley clicked off the recorder, her thoughts with Ruby and a wartime Christmas. It sounded very different to the ones she'd had when growing up. Noah was always there, of course, plus her uncle and aunt and a rota of grandparents and her great-grandmother. Christmas was her mother's favourite time of the year and was planned with military precision for maximum indulgence. It was a parade of endless food and expensive presents. One year, in an attempt to quell the extravagance, she and Noah had tried to enforce a ten-pound maximum on the present price. Her mother had sulked so much during the day, they ended up having a rerun of Christmas Day, as Lydden family tradition expected, on January the first. Ashley smiled; her mother could be hard work sometimes but she was the hub around which they all revolved. She suspected Ruby's Florrie had been much the same.

'I read the plaque that was unveiled,' Eddie said, interrupting her thoughts. 'The one in the square that states: *The bond between the soldiers of the US Army and the citizens of this town will never be broken.* Kind of makes it all the more real when you hear first-hand accounts of folk taking in GIs for Christmas.'

Ashley stowed the recorder away in her rucksack, forcing herself into the present, back to the Workshop's staff room, with a table cluttered with mugs and a fridge humming to itself in the background. 'It was a kind thing to do,' she said stiffly. 'I'm sure it was replicated across the town, if not also the country. Christmas has a way of bringing everyone together.' She bit her lip. It had certainly brought Eddie and Bree together. Shoving the ungracious thought away, she added, 'And it was incredibly thoughtful of Chet and Glenn to worry about taking Florrie's rations. They must have been nice boys.'

'Yup.' He sighed. 'Wish I could find out more about my grandfather. No one seems to know anything about him.'

'Are you sure he was billeted here?'

'Pretty sure. He was with the company that was here in Berecombe. I know the 16th were in Lyme Regis and a few were put up in Parnham Hall over Bridport way.' He gave a short laugh. 'Guess that's where they put the top brass.'

'If what Noah says is true about the numbers, the area must have been swamped with GIs,' Ashley suggested gently. She could see it was bothering him. 'Maybe he was in one of the outlying villages? Have you been in touch with the regimental contact Noah mentioned?' Now she'd been in Eddie's presence for a whole two hours, it felt a little easier talking to him. Besides, despite what had or hadn't happened between them, she genuinely wanted to help.

'Yeah. He's getting back to me. It's all taking a while, though.'

'I'm sure it was a chaotic time.'

Eddie nodded. 'Yup. Must have been. I just hoped I'd be able to tell Mom some human detail. You know, like we've just heard. She'd love to know her pa was looked after at Christmas. If there's one holiday she loves, it's Christmas.'

'My mum, too.' Ashley smiled at him and something reconnected between them.

He reached into his jacket pocket. 'Speaking of presents... Although it's not the holiday season and this isn't, strictly speaking, a present – more a necessity – I got you this.' He handed over a package wrapped in glittery blue paper. 'I saw it in a vintage shop in Exeter and thought it was just about damn perfect. Well, open it and you'll see.'

Ashley peeled away the wrapping paper, ripped off the tissue underneath and gasped. Revealed was a bicycle bell, an old-fashioned one, large and with a prominent lever. But better still, it was painted the exact same shade as her bike. She held it in her palm as if it was a precious jewel. 'It's perfect.' She smiled at him, eyes shining. 'Thank you so much, Eddie.'

'I figured that if you're cycling around Berecombe, you might need to warn people you're coming. I've seen the way folk jaywalk round this town.'

'You have no idea,' she said warmly. 'I'll put it on tonight.' She gave it an experimental ding. 'Ooh, nice and loud.'

'I tested it in the shop,' Eddie said solemnly. 'Several times. Think I drove them wild. "It's got to be right," I said to the guy. "Got to be good and loud."'

She rewrapped it and put it carefully into the side pocket of her rucksack. She was touched. It was a thoughtful present. She couldn't help but think back to the last present a man had given her: a gold chain. Piers had boasted it had cost an arm and a leg, completely missing the point that a handmade pair of earrings off a local craft stall was much more her style. They'd really had very little in common, she mused. Gazing covertly at

Eddie as he gathered up the tea things to put by the sink, she wondered how much she had in common with him and whether it mattered. She still craved his touch, but physical lust was no basis on which to build a relationship. Not one that had the potential to go the distance. Staring at his wide shoulders and sexy back as he ran hot water into the sink, she thought, had Bree not been on the scene, she might have taken the chance to find out.

Getting up, she said, 'Leave those. I'll do them afterwards. Would you like a grand tour?'

He dried his hands on the tea towel, looking surprised at the friendly overture. 'I would love one.'

She showed him the ceramics room, where several potter's wheels had been installed with a kiln at one end. She pointed out the shelves of misshapen objects. 'Students' work,' she explained on a laugh. 'Trust me, throwing a pot isn't as easy as it looks.' They toured the tutorial rooms and the large space where Ken taught graffiti art.

'These are cool,' Eddie said, admiring the vast boards.

'They are good, but you certainly know when one of these workshops is on. The spray paint reeks. We have to open up all the doors and windows.' She led him next door into the white exhibition space. 'And this is where we're going to hold Jake's show.'

'It's so great,' he said, looking around. 'The whole place is really great. If you don't mind me saying, it looks a bit run-down outside but it's like a different world in here.'

Ashley smiled ruefully. 'That's the next bid for funding. Improve the outside. When Ken set the place up, he wanted to concentrate on the inside first, and getting the right equipment. He's only just got his own studio sorted. Jed Henville helped get the funding for it. Jed's married to Millie, of Millie Vanilla's Café fame, and is the guy to go to for funding. Apparently, he knows all the right people and how to work the system. I think I can hear Ruby and Zoe in Ken's studio. Want to see?'

'You bet.'

They walked in to see Ruby, Ken and Zoe crowded around Jake's easel. Jake was sitting in front of it, looking harassed.

As he heard them come in, he turned and spread his hands as a plea for help. 'I'm being mobbed here. I keep saying I don't want your portrait to be seen until it's finished.'

'But we insisted,' Ruby added. 'I haven't got long enough to wait around. Might not live that long. And if this young man wants to paint me, I want to see an example of his work.'

'You're being a bit unfair,' Ashley protested. 'Jake

hates his work being seen until it's finished. And you could have looked at some of his other portraits – most are here waiting to be hung for his show.'

'Yes, but they wouldn't have been of someone we know,' Ruby said, her eyes gleaming with mischief. 'I want to have a look before I makes my mind up. Don't want my picture to have three noses and fourteen eyes.'

'Besides,' Ken added, 'I don't hold with all this pretentious claptrap. Come on, let's have a look, boy. No room for artistic temperament in this studio, my friend. Especially if it potentially stands in the way of getting you another commission.'

Ashley felt desperately sorry for Jake. Going to his side, she put a hand on his shoulder. He looked hounded. 'Aw, come on guys, have some respect,' she urged them.

Jake gazed up at her in gratitude and put his hand over hers. 'Thanks, Ashley.'

Ruby wasn't to be so easily thwarted. With his attention diverted, in a gesture so swift it belied her age, she whipped off the tatty material that was covering Ashley's portrait.

A collective 'ooh' rippled around the small crowd.

'What?' Ashley said and went to stand in front of it. Clasping a hand to her throat, she let out a long breath. 'Oh my.'

'He's caught you perfectly,' Eddie murmured, gazing at it intently.

The painting, although clearly unfinished, was recognisably her. Although not naturalistic in style, with great slabs of paint revealing the lights in her hair and on the side of her face turned to the window, something indefinable had been captured. Ashley could see pain, the legacy of her accident, her insecurities and painful lack of confidence. She gasped. She had been stripped bare, more naked than if he'd painted her without clothes. 'It's very good,' she muttered lamely.

'Good?' Ken exploded. 'It's bloody genius. My God, Jake, you've aced it, my friend. What a talent and a half. It'll be the star of the show!'

Jake flipped the cover back over. 'That'll be for me and Ashley to decide,' he said mulishly. 'When it's finished.'

Ashley went back to stand next to him in a show of solidarity, aware of Eddie staring.

'That's me decided,' Ruby said in triumph. 'Young man, you can paint me like your French girls. With or without clothes. I'm not fussed!'

Chapter Sixteen

'She said what?' Petra giggled.

'She wants Jake to paint her quite possibly in the nude,' Ashley answered.

'Good old Ruby. I hope I'm like her when I'm that age. What a cutie!'

'Poor old Jake,' Ashley said feelingly.

'Hey, let's not be ageist about how old flesh looks.'

'It wasn't that I was thinking of. It was him coping with Ruby as a sitter.'

They laughed.

Petra put an arm around her friend and hugged her. 'Thanks for coming along tonight. You're a star. I really appreciate the support.'

They were sitting on the edge of the stage in

Berecombe's little theatre by the sea, The Regent, dangling their feet like eight-year-olds.

'Do you think many will turn up?' Ashley asked. It was the inaugural meeting of Petra's community choir.

'I've no idea. Tonight's an experiment.'

'What made you begin one?' Ashley asked curiously. 'Haven't you got enough on your plate?'

'You could say that, but it's something I've always wanted to set up, and Berecombe, with its famous community spirit, has got to be the place to try. I've always really admired those military wives' choirs and I hero-worship Gareth Malone. Not that I see myself as him, of course,' she added hastily, 'but singing makes me feel so good, I want to share that with others. Singing in a group is fabulously uplifting. You can escape whatever's troubling you.'

Ashley looked around at the theatre's dark, moody interior. 'It's a big space to fill if you don't get many coming.'

'We'll stay on the stage if that's the case. And maybe meet in the café another time if the numbers are low. But Mike Love's offered me the theatre for nothing tonight, so I thought I'd give it a try.'

'It's a bit shabby.'

'Get you, Little Miss Positive! Theatres always look shabby when there's nothing going on,' Petra said, refusing to be deflated. 'They depend on people to bring them to life.' She looked up. 'And at least the ceiling's been fixed. Apparently, there was a bad leak last year. They ended up performing outside in the square.'

'The square's lovely. It made the perfect backdrop for the veterans' afternoon tea.'

'But the acoustics in here are better,' Petra insisted. 'And we've got the bar area to make tea and coffee in the break. It's also more contained. I've a feeling it might be like herding cats until I get them sorted.' She elbowed Ashley. 'You're a right ray of sunshine tonight. What's the matter?'

Ashley couldn't answer. She didn't know why, but the empty theatre was giving her the creeps. It reminded her of when she used to go into school to work during the summer holidays. The same expectant, hushed atmosphere, the same feeling of not knowing what was in the shadowy corners. 'I'm not sure.' She shook herself. 'Maybe I still haven't got over Jake painting my soul and exposing it to the world.'

'Your portrait's that good? Can't wait to see it.'

'It's fine, if you don't mind your insides being ripped out and put on display.'

'Then maybe what you need is a good old singsong.' Petra slid off the stage and put a hand up to Ashley to help her. Turning at the sound of voices at the door, she added, 'And I believe here come our first punters.'

In all, about thirty turned up. Petra was thrilled. She ran through a few things before they began, explaining it was all about fun and having a good time, and not about singing perfectly.

'Don't you need a piano?' Biddy barked out.

'We could use a piano but it isn't necessary. We can sing to soundtracks.'

'Can we sing some new stuff?' Zoe asked.

'I'm happy for suggestions of things to try. I draw the line at opera, though.'

'I draw the line at opera too,' Millie protested.

'Oh, I adore opera,' said a woman Ashley didn't know. She'd introduced herself as Marti Cavendish. 'In fact, I considered a career in it. I've been told I have quite the voice.'

Biddy harrumphed loudly. 'Balderdash,' she said, not quietly enough.

'Are you sure you should be here, Millie?' Amy from the bookshop asked in concern. 'You look fit to burst.'

'I've tried everything to get this baby out,' Millie sighed, rubbing her enormous bump. 'Hot baths, curry, all the usual tricks. So tonight, I'm trying to sing on a contraction.'

Ennis Senior, the only man present, put his hand up. 'I'm a qualified first aider,' he offered, in a quavering voice. 'It comes in handy down the allotments now and again. I can help if push comes to shove.' Then he blushed as he realised what he'd said.

Beryl hooted. 'If push comes to shove we'll all rally round, my lovely.' She looked at the assembled group. 'There's enough experience here. I've had three myself.'

'I'm another with three notches on the maternity bedpost, bab,' Tessa Tizzard put in. 'But poor old Ken was down at the business end. I stayed well away at the head of the bed.'

Petra let the group laugh and then called them to order. 'Tonight is an experiment,' she said. 'For you to try it to see if you like it, for us to test out the venue, and for me to hear what you've got. It's about enthusiasm and joy in singing, not about being the best tenor or soprano.'

Marti looked put out.

'Bet you anything Marti Cavendish only comes back if she gets a solo,' Amy whispered in Ashley's ear. 'I know her from Book Club. Likes to play the diva.'

Ashley grinned back and began to reply, when they were interrupted by Arthur, Biddy's husband, who bustled in.

'Hope we're not late. Thought we'd bolster the male contingent. I've dragged these two in as well.' He was followed by Noah and Eddie.

'Brilliant,' Petra said. 'That brings our male count up to four. Thanks, Arthur. Could you men stand together at Ashley and Amy's end?'

Eddie raised his brows comically and gave a sort of 'What could I do?' shrug at Ashley. Everyone shuffled up and the evening's singing began.

During the break Ashley took her coffee outside to grab some fresh air. She leaned against the wall, which gave onto the view across the bay. To the east she could see pinpricks of light at Charmouth and a car's headlights as it swooped up and down the coast road. To the west Berecombe promenade's white lights glittered in the dusky evening light. It was that magical time of the year when it didn't get properly dark. Warmth from the day hung heavy in the air and Ashley drank in the slabs of red and gold streaking across the sky, deepening into violet in the east and sinking into the sea. She took a few pictures with her phone but was disappointed it didn't fully capture the glory. She concentrated, instead, on committing it to memory as she longed to paint it.

'Another magnificent Berecombe view,' said a voice at her side. It was Eddie. 'I've brought you out a cupcake.

Millie brought them with her but only just remembered. Think she said something about baby brain.'

She turned away from one entrancing view to another. Eddie was all warm, dark shadow and her senses tingled with longing. 'Thank you.' She took the cake off him, her fingers accidentally touching his, an electrical charge of desire bolting through her. 'She's done well to stay,' she said, trying for the mundane. Eddie had stood next to her during the singing and his mellow tenor had thrilled her.

'Yeah. Jed's collected her now. She was flagging. Think the *Grease* medley was to blame. One step too far after "A tisket, a tasket, I've lost my yellow basket".'

'I know. Where did Petra dig that one up from? It was a laugh, though.' Ashley let a giggle escape. 'Especially when we tried singing it in rounds.' She looked around quickly to see if anyone else was outside but saw they were alone. 'I think Petra's got her work cut out with Biddy.'

'Got a deeper voice than any of the men.'

'Certainly louder.'

'And every one a bum note.'

'Perhaps we're being a bit mean, though. She does suffer from hearing loss.'

'Oh jeez – yes, perhaps we are. I always forget that about Biddy.' He pulled a face. 'Most of the time I'm too scared of her to have any kind of conversation. She's a game girl to have a go, in that case.'

'Think Biddy has definitely been a game girl in the past.' Ashley laughed again. 'I enjoyed it. Hadn't realised singing could be so much fun. But what on earth are you doing here? For the life of me, it's the last place I thought I'd see you.'

'Don't tell me. Me too. There I was, having a quiet pint of warm ale in the Old Harbour with Noah, when Arthur comes in recruiting. Noah felt obliged, as a pillar of the community.'

'And to garner possible points with Petra.'

'And to garner possible points with Petra,' he conceded on a laugh. 'There is that. So, I faced the choice of drinking on my own or coming along. It's been a blast.' He broke off a piece of cake and ate it. 'Good cake too. Preferable to a night alone in Exeter.'

'No Bree?' Ashley could have bitten off her tongue. Why did she have to mention the woman's name when she and Eddie had been getting on so well?

He didn't seem fazed. 'Hadn't you heard? She's back in the States. Had to get back to work sometime.'

'Oh. Do you miss her?' *God, Ashley. Big foot. Mouth. Insert.*

Eddie shrugged but didn't answer. For a few moments they ate their cakes in silence, then he crumpled up the paper case and said, 'I'm not going to repeat what I've explained about me and Bree and the baby. I can appreciate you finding it hard to accept. Can't say I'm happy about being only your friend, but if that's what you want... If it means spending time with you, Ashley, I'll go with that. And we seem to be getting along okay lately.'

Ashley caught her breath. Eddie's face was in shadow and she couldn't read his expression, but the warmth in his low voice had want racing through her. It was as if now she'd denied herself, she wanted him all the more. The space between them vibrated with desire and she ached to hold him. Need made her crave to press herself against him. Hardly daring to breathe, she reached out, putting tentative, exploring fingers to his chest, feeling his pulse quicken and leap. She heard him snatch a breath in surprise and her hand, seemingly of its own accord, inched up to the skin at the opening of his shirt, to the hairs that sprang there. Slid further to the warm smooth skin of his neck and slowly, oh so slowly into his hair, tugging on it and then snatching his mouth down onto hers. A sigh of release echoed from her into him. He tasted of chocolate cupcake and was sweet with sugar and desire. His sandalwood scent filled her senses.

After a second's hesitation, he groaned her name, banded his arms around her and brought her to him roughly. His mouth trailed a blaze along her skin, making her cry out when he found the sensitive niche at the base of her throat. Turning her so that she backed against the wall, the wide-open sky and crimson sea a forgotten backdrop, he whispered, 'Ashley, what are you doing to me?' against her heated skin, his voice low and guttural with desire. He kissed her until she was mad for more.

She grabbed his hand, putting it between her legs so that it cupped her over her jeans. It was as if she had opened the floodgates of her desire, her want. Still needing more, she ripped open her shirt and pulled his mouth to her breast. Her head lolled back in ecstasy as his tongue found her nipple, his lips surrounding her flesh, sucking and licking until she was sent crazy. She bucked into him urgently, desperate for him. Desperate for some relief from the sweet torture. All she could see was red and black and spiralling need.

And then Eddie stopped. Pulled away. 'What are we doing, Ashley?' he panted. 'Is this your idea of being friends? 'Cos I'm getting mighty confused here.'

Slowly Ashley came back into herself and blinked at him, trying to see him properly in the dark. She'd been so close to coming, it was all she had focused on. She'd forgotten they were in the courtyard outside the theatre. Had forgotten they were in public and could be seen by anyone strolling past. Her back felt sore and scraped from the rough wall behind; her sex throbbed, unsatisfied. A cold breeze blew across her hot skin and, to her shock, she realised her shirt was hanging open, exposing her breasts to the world. Buttoning it back up with trembling fingers, she tried to speak but couldn't trust her voice. What had got into her? Tucking her shirt into her jeans, she began, 'Eddie, I—'

He wiped the back of his hand across his mouth. 'This isn't fair.' He pointed an angry finger. 'I've made my feelings clear. I know what I want, I want a relationship with you. But you're blowing hot and cold – what's all that about? If it's just sex you want, then fine, you go find it elsewhere. Sure, I'd bust a gut to sleep with you, but I want more than that. Just sex ain't on my agenda, so make your mind up about what *you* want, Ash.' He scrubbed a furious hand through his hair. 'Jeez, don't bother explaining. I'm outta here.'

'Eddie, I—' she tried again but her voice came out only as a hoarse whisper and was snatched away by the sea breeze. 'Don't go. I'm sorry.'

He shook his head and put up his hands in defence. Then he walked off, striding across the cobbled square and into a night flaming with a sunset. Her chest heaved, every sense aglow and frustrated. Whipping round to face the sunset, she hid her face in her hands, grinding her teeth in mortification. What the hell was she doing? She was losing her mind. How could she have jumped on him like that? She never did things like that! Why couldn't she rein in her feelings for this man? She laid her head on the cool stone wall, wailing silently. Why was it all so complicated? Turning to search the blackness that had swallowed him up, she wondered how she'd ever face the man again.

Chapter Seventeen

'What about here?' Jake suggested.

It was a hot July day with a cloudless sky and a gentle breeze. With the beach and town heaving, Jake and Ashley had decided to seek some peace and quiet to paint and had wandered along the river to the converted mill. A curve in the river created a pebble beach in the shade of some willows and was the perfect spot. The occasional dog walker passed by or a family on the way to the seafront but, other than that, they had it to themselves.

Jake helped Ashley over the rough ground, set up a couple of stools and then left her to organise her painting kit. As usual, she'd brought only what she could carry in her rucksack so it didn't take too long. She noted Jake had brought with him a portable easel and grinned to herself. Maybe that's what divided the professional from the amateur.

The time passed and they didn't talk much, lulled into a companionable silence by the blanket of heat. Ashley concentrated on painting a corner of the mill, the curve of glistening water, and three willow trees dipping their tendrils into the river.

Eventually she put her sketch pad down and eased a kink out of her shoulder. Taking off her sun hat, she lifted her hair, which lay heavy and hot on her neck. Fanning herself, she became aware of Jake, to her right, drawing furiously. As she glanced over he looked up and scrutinised her in a way that made her sure she was his subject.

'Didn't you have enough time to look at me in the studio?' she asked. She'd sat for him a couple of times more, during which time he'd taken yet more photos on his phone for future reference. He'd said it was nearly finished and wouldn't need her to sit for him again.

Jake turned his pad around for her to see. It revealed a completely new drawing and showed her stretching out her shoulders, one hand under her hair. It was full of dappled sunlight and sensuous lines.

Ashley laughed in embarrassment. 'That's not really me. It's so sexy.'

'Don't you see yourself as sexy?'

She closed the lid of her water-colour tin carefully. 'No comment.'

'I think you're the sexiest woman I've ever met.'

'Don't.'

'Don't what?'

'Flirt.'

'I'm not flirting,' he protested. 'It's true. What makes you even sexier is that you're completely unaware of it.'

Their eyes met.

'You're my muse. But I'd like you to be more,' he said breathily, his blue eyes glinting dangerously through the dark lashes.

'I'm sure you would, but I have no intention of being added to your list of conquests.'

He laughed. 'Notches on the bedpost? I'm not like that.'

'Aren't you? Either way, I'm not interested, Jake. I like you as a friend, as a painting companion; nothing more. Besides, weren't you flirting outrageously with Zoe only the other day?'

He shrugged.

'You can't turn it off, can you?'

He shrugged again and spread his hands, making her giggle. A man was strolling along the riverside path and the sound caught his attention. He stopped for a second, put up a hand in greeting and then carried on walking, his long strides carrying him away before she had time to respond. Ashley's breath stuck in her throat. It was Eddie. She felt Jake's eyes on her, stripping her emotions bare, as usual.

'Ah, so that's it.'

She became very busy putting away her painting stuff. 'I don't know what you mean.'

'You know precisely what I mean.' Jake folded up his easel. 'So, what's stopping you?'

'What's stopping me what?'

'Pursuing the man you've obviously got the hots for.'

'You do talk a load of old rubbish sometimes. I do not have the hots, as you so quaintly put it, for Eddie McQueen.'

'Yeah? Bite me.'

Ashley shoved her pad into the rucksack and gave in. 'His not-so-ex-girlfriend is having his baby.'

'So?'

'So?' She rounded on him. 'I don't want to have anything to do with him.' The memory of how she'd kissed him outside the theatre the other night made her face glow with the lie. 'I do not want to have a relationship with Eddie McQueen.' A duck, alarmed at her raised voice, squawked and flew off.

'Aw hell, Ashley. Who's talking about a relationship? Just get in there, maid, and give him one. Cure the itch.'

'And that's what you'd do with me, is it? Cure the itch.'

Jake gave her a penetrating stare. 'Nah. With you once would never be enough. Once I'd had you, I'd want to go back time and time again. Think if I got you to scratch my itch, it would just multiply.'

Ashley shivered. He was a deeply attractive man. Quite possibly completely amoral but, with that smooth dark skin, curling hair and those devastating eyes, as blue as the Cornish sea, you couldn't argue he wasn't drop-dead gorgeous. Add on his astonishing star appeal, and she felt herself go weak. A night with him would be memorable. It would be like sleeping with Picasso. But she couldn't do it. Wouldn't do it. No matter how tempted she was. She blew out a breath.

'But that's what might happen if I slept with Eddie,' she countered. It was true. Once she'd had a taste of Eddie she didn't think she'd ever want to give him up. And that's what made him so dangerous.

'Ah.' Jake stood, slung the strap of his easel across his back and added, 'Then you have to make a decision.'

'Tell me about it,' she said miserably. 'The trouble is, when I'm around him my head's telling me one thing and my heart the other.'

'Which one wins?' He seemed genuinely curious.

'The last time?' Ashley pulled a rueful face. 'I'd say

my hormones won the battle. Not sure I can look him in the face ever again. He hasn't come back to choir since. Think I've frightened him off.'

'Is that where it happened?' he said on a grin. 'Got to say, I like the sound of your choir. Might join.'

'It was during the break, Jake. I was outside enjoying the sunset.'

'And you ended up enjoying Eddie too?' He cackled.

'Glad you find it so funny. I had to go back in for the second half and make up some excuse that he'd had to go for his train. I don't think anyone believed me.'

'Well, they wouldn't, if you went in looking like your face had been snogged off.'

Ashley stood and pulled her rucksack over her shoulders. 'The more this conversation carries on, the more I think you have in common with Zoe. And she's barely twenty.'

He came to her and folded up her stool. 'I just don't see the problem. If you like him, go for it. See what happens. Life is for living, Ash. You never know when it'll be your last day on this planet.' He gave her a measured look. 'I would have thought you, of all people, would know that.'

'You know about my accident?' she asked, taken aback.

'I didn't. Until your face just told me. Reckon you've got to make the most of your time here.'

'You might have a point.'

''Course I do.' He turned to walk up to the path.

'Jake.'

Twisting back, he held out a hand to help her. 'Yep?'

'You descended from the fairy folk or something?'

He grinned wickedly. 'Nah.' Taking her hand in his firm, warm, paint-covered grip, he added, 'Reckon my dad was a Cornish pixie, though.'

As she smiled up at him, she noticed the sun had brought out freckles across his nose. It made him appear less the amoral alpha male, less of a painting genius and more boyish. And even more sexy.

Chapter Eighteen

On the afternoon of Jake's exhibition, Ruby rang Ashley asking if they could record another memories session in The Workshop.

'I'm using my new mobile,' the old woman explained excitedly. 'I've got the hang of it now. It's ever so handy. I just thought it would save me a journey if I do a session with you on the same day. I can get all dressed up, have a chat with you, pop by the exhibition, grab me free glass of wine and tootle off home. Be back in my bed by nine.'

When Ashley said she couldn't guarantee Eddie's presence, for once it didn't seem to matter. Relieved she didn't have to face him, she was waiting in the staff room, a pot of tea brewing in readiness when Biddy dropped Ruby off.

'I'm just off to see Millie's baby,' Biddy said. 'Did you

hear she's had a girl? Named her Edie. Isn't that pretty?' She swooped threateningly close to Ashley. 'Don't wear Ruby out,' she whispered. 'She's not been too well these past few days.'

The problem was, Biddy's whisper was more of a yell and Ruby overheard. 'I'm as fit as a flea and twice as lively,' she protested. 'It were that cream sauce on the fish the other night. It was too rich.'

'More likely the second helping of apple pie and custard you had.'

Ruby winked at Ashley. 'Got to take your pleasures where you can find them at my age.'

'And if I deliver you back to your daughter in a box, the pleasures in my life will come to an abrupt end,' Biddy replied waspishly. 'I'll be back later for the exhibition. Bye, both.' And, with that, she swept out, her dog Elvis scampering in her wake.

Ashley settled Ruby in a chair and poured her a cup of tea. 'Aren't you and Biddy getting on?' she asked, concerned.

'Me and old Biddy?' Ruby's brows rose in astonishment and her face creased into lines. 'Get on like a house on fire. Why'd you ask?'

Ashley hid a grin. 'Oh, no reason.' For a second they sipped tea in companionable silence, then, with a glance at the door, she said, 'Biddy's never without her poodle, is she? I've always wondered exactly what a deaf-assistance dog does.'

'What, little Elvis? Oh, he's a dear. Lets Biddy know when there's someone at the door, brings the phone to her when it rings. He's even been trained to jump on the bed if the smoke alarm goes off at night. Mind you, Arthur does a lot of that for her now.'

'Yes, I suppose he does.' Ashley smiled, an image of the placid Arthur jumping on the bed invading her imagination. 'It's rather touching that they've found love at their mature age. I don't think they've been married all that long.'

'Don't think they have, an' all.'

Ashley pushed the recorder to the middle of the table. 'What did you want to talk about, Ruby? You seemed keen to do a session.'

Ruby drew in a breath. She put down her cup carefully. 'I been thinking about Jimmy. He's been on my mind a lot. Maybe it's because I'm here in Berecombe again.'

'I enjoyed the last session and hearing about Christmas and the GIs leaving. It was very moving.'

'It was.' Ruby's eyes misted over, then she changed the subject abruptly. 'It's nice about little Edie, isn't it? A new baby in the world always gives hope.'

Ashley wondered where this was going. The last

thing she wanted to discuss was babies. The world seemed full of pregnant women. Everyone was having a baby. Everyone except her.

'Funny, haven't thought about all this for years. Got on with my life. Tried to forget all about Jimmy and Chet and Berecombe. Married my Alan. Had Serena. I told you, didn't I, that I named her Serena, as she was supposed to bring me some peace? She was the baby to replace the one I lost.'

'You lost a baby?' Ashley's breath caught in her throat.

Ruby blinked. 'Didn't I tell you? I thought I wrote about it in the letter I sent. You did get it, lovie, didn't you? The letter.'

Ashley nodded.

'I fell for Chet's baby.'

'Yes, you wrote to me about that. And you've told me how Jimmy broke the news that Chet had died on D-Day and that Jimmy wanted to marry you, but you returned to London. You didn't mention what happened to the baby.'

Ruby's lips worked as she sat in silence. Ashley refilled her cup and pushed it nearer. 'I don't have to record this, if you'd rather I didn't,' she said gently. 'In fact, you don't have to tell me anything, Ruby. It's your history. It isn't any of my business, really.'

The old woman took a sip of tea. 'I like talking to you. I like doing this recording lark. I want it recorded for posterity. For folk to know what it was like. Oh, Ashley, it were a vivid time to be alive. Not easy, mind, but, I don't know, *concentrated*. I lived more in the few years I lived here in Berecombe than in the whole of the rest of my life.' She grimaced. 'I don't mean to say I haven't enjoyed the rest of my life – I loved Alan until the day he died and I love Serena, but it was all more... oh, I don't know... humdrum, I suppose, after the war. Working, saving up for a little holiday, getting tea on the table, sorting out Serena's problems and then her children's, seeing her through her divorce. Life, I suppose.' She shot Ashley a teary look, 'And they say you never forget your first love, don't they?'

'They do.' Ashley put her hand over Ruby's and squeezed it gently. 'If you really feel up to it then, tell me about the baby.'

Ruby sucked in another calming breath. 'Not much to tell. Not really. I lived with Florrie and Jimmy until that August. The baby was just about starting to show by then, if you looked close enough, and Jimmy was putting on the pressure for me to give him an answer. In a nice way. He was concerned for me and how it looked, you see.

'One evening, we were all sitting round the radio

listening to Jimmy Dorsey. Florrie was always keen on a big band. I was feeling a bit teary on account of them playing "When They Ask About You", as me and Chet had danced to that one. I was just about to get up to make a cuppa to distract me when I felt something inside me. I felt something move! I held my breath and put my hand on my belly. It was the baby. I could feel the baby move.

'I looked across at the others but they hadn't noticed anything. Florrie was half asleep and Jimmy was reading the paper. I watched him as he read; he was frowning over something or other. A good man. A kind one and he loved me, but I knew then I couldn't marry him. Not with another man's baby inside me. And I didn't love him. Not like he wanted me to. He was a brother, not a husband. I knew I'd break his heart if I married him, somewhere down the line. I knew we wouldn't be happy, so I thought I might as well break his heart sooner rather than later. It was as if the baby was telling me something with that first kick.

'The following morning, I told Florrie I was going back to me mam. Back to London. I told her some half-cock tale about how, with a baby on the way, I was needing my own mother. Well, I hadn't needed my ma for five years and I knew damn well what her reaction was going to be when she found out my condition, but I didn't let on to Florrie. I packed a bag and got the bus to the station that same day.'

'Did you say goodbye to Jimmy?'

Ruby looked away. 'Blurted something or other out, explaining that I couldn't marry him, and ran off. I know it was cowardly but I was that mixed up. So much had happened to me in a few short months. And, in my heart of hearts, I knew I'd disappointed Jimmy. I wasn't the girl he'd idolised. I'd fallen off that pedestal good and proper. I'm not proud of what I did, I know I should have explained, but I'd run out of words. All I knew was, I wanted to get away, away from Berecombe, away from all the memories of Chet. I wanted to make a new life for me and the baby. In London.'

'Understandable.' Ashley was silent for a moment. Her own problems had been insignificant compared to Ruby's, but she understood the need to flee. To carve a new existence. It was demarcation lines again. Separating an old life from the new. Noah's accusation – that she ran out on a problem rather than tackling it head on – came back. But sometimes running was the only answer. 'You were so young, Ruby. You'd been through so much.'

Ruby nodded.

'May I ask what happened next?'

'Well, Mam went ape. Barely spoke a word to me. Mrs Wicke, from next door, fudged a job for me at a British

Restaurant. I wore big thick cardies to stop anyone guessing. London was a funny place then. Worst of the war over, but the odd V2 to contend with. They were horrible things!' She shuddered. 'We were all just waiting. Waiting for it to be finished.

'Well, maybe it was the hard work at the café, being on my feet all day, or maybe it was just meant to be. All I knew was, one night I woke up in such pain, blood all over the eiderdown. Mam fetched Mrs Howarth from over the road, on account of her having done a bit of nursing, but it was too late. I lost the baby. A little boy, it was. I cuddled him and cried and cried. We all cried. He might have been a bastard but he was an innocent. My poor little baby boy, and I'd lost him.' Ruby gave a great wailing cry. 'I'd lost the only bit of Chet I had left.'

Chapter Nineteen

There was a long silence only punctuated by Ruby's quavering sobs. Ashley pulled her chair close and put her arms around the frail old body. She could sense the woman was deep in grief, staring into the past and the awful night when she had lost her baby. Ashley didn't want to disturb her and didn't have the first idea of what to say. She couldn't imagine the heartbreak of losing a child. Instead, she rested her head on Ruby's shoulder as silent comfort.

The two women sat for some time and, when Ruby seemed calmer, Ashley made yet another pot of tea. She didn't think she'd ever be able to make tea again without seeing Ruby in one of her neat pastel-coloured twinsets, snowy white candy-floss hair, nursing a cup.

Eventually Ruby began speaking again. 'He would be

seventy-five now.' She gave a hard short laugh. 'An old man! Imagine that.'

Ashley couldn't. It was tear-jerkingly painful to think Ruby still marked the years of her son's lost life. She placed a fresh cup in front of her, desperately wishing it was something stronger. Floundering for something to say, she murmured, 'You went on to make a life. A good life. And then you had Serena.'

Ruby sat back in her chair, as if shrugging the past, and all its pain, off. 'Years later, mind. Much later. I was an old mum when I had her.' She snorted. 'Pretended she was my first. Never told Alan. Only told Serena when Alan was in his grave. Think that's why she was so awkward about me coming here and remembering. Jealous, she is, of my lost little boy. Always thinks she comes second in my affections. She was a good little girl, though. Good daughter.'

'Anyone can see she loves you very much. She's very protective. You live with her, don't you?'

Ruby nodded, blinking herself back to the present. 'Big house in Blackheath.' She snorted. 'When I was a kid that's where the posh folk lived. She's got this four-storey thing. Don't know why she wants a house so big. I've got a flat on the side. They calls it a granny flat. It's nice. Suits me. I can walk to the shops if I've a mind. View of the garden. Our Serena's got a gardener. Keeps it neat.

Doesn't stop me thinking, though. I've had a whole life in London, working, being a wife, bringing up my child. But what happened here during the war... well, that shaped me.'

'So, tell me more about Jimmy. You must have been good friends. Despite all that happened between you.' Ashley was torn. Part of her was greedy to hear more about the terrible night of the miscarriage. She calculated. It must have been a late one. Ruby must have gone through labour, only to deliver a baby that had been born dead or survived only minutes. She clamped down on her inappropriate curiosity and tried to change the subject, not wanting to upset Ruby again. 'I've always thought Jimmy sounded such a nice man. He seems to have been a real pillar in the community here. It's such a shame he didn't marry.'

Ruby's lips pursed. 'It is. He'd have made some woman a good husband. And I suppose we were good friends, in our way. He was a gawky youth when I met him. I didn't take much notice of him and then off he went to war. It was two years or more by the time he came back. He was thin and shrunken into himself, like an old man.

'One afternoon he told me what had happened to him. We'd gone for a stroll along the front, or as best we could. I was a bit nervy about being out because of the poor woman who got hit in Swanage. Sitting on a bench, we heard, minding her own business, reading a book. Jerry plane came out of nowhere and machine-gunned her.'

'Oh my God!'

'Broad daylight it was, as well. I mean, you could sort of understand bombing factories and docks and the like – I mean, that was war – but this was just spiteful. What harm was she doing?'

'Did she survive?'

'Took her off to hospital and thankfully, by all accounts, she was all right. I felt safer with Jimmy. As I said, he was like a big brother. Always looking after me. We walked along the prom here and went into the café on the front. The one you call Millie's.'

'What was it called then?'

Ruby screwed up her face. 'I'm trying to remember. It was a bit different back then, I can tell you. Tiny, it was. Woman who run it only kept it going during the war on account of the fact that she lived in the flat above, and she thought she might as well. She was called Glad or something. Her real name was Gladys Brown or... Bray, that's right, Gladys Bray. Glad was her nickname.' Ruby seemed relieved to be talking about a less emotive subject. 'Only she never was – glad, I mean,' she added with a chuckle. 'Florrie knew her quite well and said she'd never had a glad bone in her body from the day she was born.

'That day Jimmy and me had a pot of tea and a jam tart between us as a treat. I told him I was worried about getting hit from a plane and he said he'd had his bad luck for the war. Then he told me about what he'd been through. Not much detail, but enough for me to get a picture.

'He'd been waiting for a boat to collect him at Dunkirk. Well, I told you what that was like. Horrible. Shocking. There was a bit of jostling because there was a boat coming towards them. I think he said he was still on the jetty, or the Mole, I think it was called, and he saw a boy in the water. Don't know if he'd fallen off, or fallen out of another boat, or was being washed out to sea but, anyway, Jimmy jumped in. Held this kid's head above water for an hour or more until they got a boat to them.

'He got the lad onto the boat – he was only eighteen or so, Jimmy said – but there was no room for him. He had to stay in the sea for the next one. Plane must have strafed the water or something, as Jimmy said all of a sudden, the water all around him was burning, alight from the fuel on a boat that had been hit. That's when he got burned. Burned all along the jaw, down to his shoulder and across his body.

'Funnily enough, he landed in the same hospital as

the boy he'd rescued. He had a visit from him. Nice that he survived. Poor old Jimmy was in a bad way, though. Couldn't move his one arm much at first – used to tuck his hand in his pocket to hide the scar and make it a bit more comfortable, like. "What girl will want me now?" he used to say. He didn't think he could offer any woman anything, see.

'Over the next year, afore Chet and the Yanks turned up, we got closer. Used to tell me tales of being a kid in Berecombe. He had great fun, he said. Well, what child wouldn't when you'd got the beach and the sea as your playground? But I only ever thought of him as a big brother. Never realised he felt romantic about me. He never made a move, never said nothing. I suppose he didn't feel he could, what with being injured and all. I'm wondering now if he only asked me to marry him as I was damaged goods, like him, when I fell pregnant. Two lame ducks together.'

'No, I'm sure he loved you very much. He wanted to do the honourable thing by you.'

'Perhaps. He could be a funny cuss, could Jimmy. When Chet used to come to tea and I'd sit in the parlour with him, Jimmy would lurk in the back room, keeping an eye out. Warned me Yanks only wanted one thing. Trouble was, I was so innocent, I didn't know what he was on about!'

'Different times. I should think a sixteen-year-old nowadays knows everything there is to know.'

'And the rest! I've got a seventeen-year-old granddaughter. Some of the things she says! Makes my hair curl, she does. And that's when I know what she's on about.'

'I know what you mean. I taught for years and have heard all sorts from the kids and teens in my classes.' Ashley smiled. 'One thing puzzles me, though.'

'What's that, dearie?' Ruby drank her tea and said yes to another refill.

'If Jimmy was so badly injured in the war, how did he volunteer for the RNLI?'

'I don't think he was ever crew, think he did the admin, answering the phone, working in the shop. That sort of thing. I had a chat with that boy Oliver Lacey at the wake. He said they'd never let someone not physically fit go out to sea.'

'Makes sense. It's lovely that he still managed to have a rich, fulfilled life, despite his injuries.'

Ruby eyed her keenly. 'Folk can, you know.'

Ashley blushed. 'Of course they can. It's a shame this eighteen-year-old, the one Jimmy saved, didn't know about the funeral. Did Jimmy ever tell you his name?'

Ruby shook her head. 'Never. He's probably long gone by now, anyway. I'm last man standing, as Poppy, my granddaughter, likes to gleefully point out. Besides, Jimmy only talked about it that once. Very modest man, was Jimmy Larcombe. He didn't like talking about Dunkirk. Gave him nightmares.'

'Yes, I remember you saying. It's not surprising.' They sat in silence for a moment and then Ashley fanned herself with a paper serviette. She got up to open the window. 'Hot again today. How do you like the warm weather, Ruby?'

'I don't mind it. I'm always so cold it makes a change to be warm.' She cackled. 'That reminds me.'

'What of?'

'Of a hot May night.' She sighed.

'What happened?'

'That thing still on?' Ruby nodded to the recorder. 'This'll get them sitting up and taking notice.'

Ashley sat back down, intrigued. 'I can't wait to hear this!'

'It was late May, 1944,' Ruby began. 'Chet had got an inkling something was going to blow up soon. We all did. There was something in the air. Everyone was all expectant. It was hot – ooh, it was that hot! You couldn't sleep at night, not a breath of air. I was lying there, tossing and turning in me bed, when there was a rattling at the window. It was Chet! Only gone and thrown a handful of stones at the window, hadn't he? Glenn and him had bust out of camp. Reckon they thought this near the big show, no one would bother putting them on a charge and, if they did, they might get lucky and miss it all. They'd collected Iris on the way, and did I want to go for a swim? Boy, did I!

'We crept down to the front, found a gap in the barbed wire. The local boys were always finding a way through – we would have had no chance if Jerry had decided to invade; they could have walked right through! I'll never forget the feel of the water on my skin. Silky, it was. I was cool for the first time in weeks. Before I knew it, Glenn and Iris had disappeared along the beach, and me and Chet were alone. All alone in the dark. No one to disturb us. No one to see.

'Well, one thing led to another, didn't it, and we made love. First time for the both of us. We sort of half knew what we was doing, but it was a bit of a frantic fumble. I think Chet knew then he was going into something big and he might not come back. Wanted to go into battle as a man, I suppose, and I was happy to help, all right. I knew it was wrong but, on another level, it didn't feel like that at all. Felt like the most natural thing in the world. We loved each other. Then we shared a ciggie – hiding the light, of course – and fell asleep. Woke up with the dawn and the seagulls. Chet ran off – scared silly, he was, about sneaking back into camp.'

'Did he get caught?' Ashley asked gently.

'He didn't, but I did! Halfway up the stairs to the flat, I was, to find Jimmy staring down at me from the landing. That was the thing with Jimmy. He didn't say much, but one look at his face told you everything he was thinking. I knew then how he felt and what he thought about me. He made me feel ashamed. Spoiled it. I was angry with him. I didn't want to feel shame. There was no shame to be found in what me and Chet had done. I was proud I'd sent him to war knowing what a woman felt like.'

Ruby shook her head and added ruefully, 'Only did it the once, but once was enough to get me pregnant. The thing was, when I married my Alan, we tried for ten years. Funny how that goes, ain't it?' She fingered the teaspoon lying in the sugar bowl. 'Things weren't the same between me and Jimmy after that. We'd tiptoe round one another, with Florrie pestering us to tell her why. I tried to talk to him once, to explain, but he couldn't bear to be in the same room as me. That hurt. I was very fond of him.

'Then came the day the GIs shipped out, and I cried and cried. And when the news came through about the casualties and he told me Chet was dead, he warmed up to me again. Held me in his arms. We talked and drank tea all night. Used up a week's rations. He told me whatever happened, he'd look after me. Of course, I wanted to find out more about how Chet had died, but Jimmy warned me not to. Said I didn't want to know the details about war. "War's not pretty," he said. After what he'd told me about Dunkirk, I suppose he had a point.'

After chewing her lip for a second, Ruby unclasped the silver locket from around her neck. 'Here, this is what me and Chet looked like. I cut them small so they would fit inside.' With bent, arthritic fingers she prised open the locket and held it out.

Ashley took it, holding the necklace like the precious link to the past that it was, and gazed at the tiny black and white photographs. On the left was Ruby, her famous hair cascading around her shoulders, her eyes wide and innocent. She was very pretty. Chet, in uniform, sported a savage crew cut, and was handsome with a sharp jawline. He looked painfully young and Ashley was saddened to realise it may well have been the last photograph taken of him. 'Beautiful,' she whispered and handed it back to Ruby, a lump in her throat. 'Just beautiful.'

Chapter Twenty

After Biddy had collected Ruby to take her for a quick bite before the exhibition, Ashley found herself sitting alone in the staff room, staring into space. The woman had lived more of a life in the war years than most had in an entire lifetime. The same could be said of Chet, except his was cut cruelly short. She made a note to ask Ruby his full name and to try to find out exactly how he died.

'What are you doing skulking in here?' Ken burst into the room, his energy filling it and making her jump. 'Come on, get your glad rags on, my friend, we have a big night in front of us.'

Thirty minutes later, said glad rags on, Ashley stood in the exhibition space feeling disorientated, trying to concentrate on a twenty-first-century art exhibition and not linger on ghosts of memories from World War Two. She was nervous. She'd worked hard on getting it just right; it had almost taken her mind off the complication that was Eddie. Having only previously organised school art exhibitions, this was the first time she'd pulled one together for a professional, and she was all too aware of how much this could mean to Jake's career.

'Stop overthinking it.' Ken handed her a glass, reading her mind. 'Only prosecco, but some Dutch courage. You've done a great job, Ash. Relax and enjoy the evening.'

She took the glass and sipped. 'Thanks, Ken, but I'm not sure I'll relax until all this is over. It's like hosting a party, but one which could be make or break for one of the guests.'

Ken laughed. 'If it happens for Jake, it happens. If it doesn't, well, we'll think of another tactic.'

'Remind me, who are these dealers you've invited?'

'Freya and Damon? Freya owns a gallery in SW1 and Damon works for a high-end auctioneers.'

Ashley gulped down more prosecco. 'Blimey.'

'They're only people. If it helps, imagine them naked.'

'Not helping, Ken. Not helping at all.'

He saluted her with his glass. 'You're looking good, try to feel as good on the inside. It's all smoke and mirrors in the end.'

'Thanks.' Ashley tugged at the dress she'd chosen. She'd had little idea what to wear and even less choice. She'd spotted it in the only clothes shop Berecombe possessed. It was a fairly safe black number but with a plunging neckline that dipped far lower than she'd first thought. Wanting to cover up her cleavage, she'd added a heavy necklace of blue-green sea glass bought in one of Berecombe's tourist shops.

'Uh-oh, here come the first punters.' Ken stiffened at the sound of Zoe greeting someone at the main door. 'Got your sales stickers at the ready?'

She held out the sheet of red dots.

'And you remember how to record any sales in the book?'

She nodded, her lips quirking. 'Think I can just about manage it.'

'Sorry, my lovely, didn't mean to patronise you, just want things to go well for the boy.'

'So do I.'

He blew out a breath, looking harassed. 'There's me telling you not to get stressed, and I think I'm the one feeling the nerves.'

Ashley looked around, at the chairs and tables set up

in strategic places, at Louis Tizzard waiting with a tray of tiny posh snacks, at Jake's magnificent paintings glowing with their jewel-like colours against the pure white walls. 'Think we've done all we can. It looks great in here.'

'Then we're all set.' He went to meet Biddy, Arthur and Ruby, who, predictably, were the first to arrive. 'Biddy,' he said as he reached forward to kiss her on the cheek. 'Welcome. Do help yourself to a glass of fizz from Sean here. And middle son will be around with canapés soon.'

Ashley took herself to a quiet corner of the room and people watched. One thing she'd worried about was guests promising to come but not turning up. Clearly this wasn't going to be the case. Soon, the space was full of people milling about, sipping free booze and nibbling the chicken katsu curry Louis was serving. She smiled. He wasn't doing too bad a job. Whereas Sean, Ken's oldest son, was shy to the point of being monosyllabic, Louis had inherited his father's charm and easy manner. He'd also, according to Ken, squeezed them for double the normal rate of pay.

She watched as Jake, another confident charmer, worked the room. He was born to the role, greeting guests with a handshake or kiss, talking animatedly about his work. He was also downing glass after glass of prosecco, which was worrying. They all needed him to be on the ball and professional tonight. It was his chance to wow the room.

Turning to her, as if sensing her watching, he came over. 'Good turnout.' He clinked her glass with his own.

'It is. And you're doing a great job.' She surveyed him over the rim of her prosecco. 'You've scrubbed up well,' she said mischievously. He had. Wearing a pair of tight black jeans and a sapphire blue shirt, which made his eyes blaze, he looked good. 'Very much the promising young artist.' His star power was mesmerising and Ashley felt the pull into his orbit.

He grinned. 'Let's hope this lot think so too. Any sales yet?'

She blinked and shook her head. 'Too early, I think. Let's get them a little more mellow with plonk before we start on the sales drive.'

His eyes dropped to her cleavage. He reached out and lifted the heavy necklace, with fingers that still bore paint. 'Beautiful,' he murmured, caressing the stones. Laying it back on her neck, his fingertips strayed to just under the neckline of her dress, his hand excitingly calloused on her skin. 'Thanks, Ashley, for organising this.' Giving her an intense stare, he added, 'For everything.'

Breath caught in her throat. God, he was sexy. His genius was sexy. 'Ken did most of it. I just tagged along.' It came out on a ragged breath. Half of her wanted to get away. Most of her was hypnotised.

'Stop being modest. I know that's not true.' He inched closer. 'Most of all, thank you for being you, for being my muse. You've woken something in me that I thought a cynical world had beaten out.'

Ashley's throat closed. With his richly curling hair and thickly lashed eyes, his appeal was extraordinary. If there was ever a man born to flirt, it was Jake Tremayne. What would it be like to sleep with him? To get close to that virtuosity? Did he make love with the same skill as he painted? The questions flitted across her imagination like quicksilver and brought her up short. She'd never seen herself as a particularly sexual person but, what with Eddie and now this lust for Jake, she was having to reassess. Maybe a quick fling with him wasn't such a bad idea? Hadn't he said it was like scratching an itch? And at least, as far as she knew, he came unencumbered with complicated baggage. Unlike Eddie. And it was clear he wanted her. Unlike Piers. Humour curled inside her; she knew exactly what Petra would say. She knew exactly what Petra would do. Her chin rose involuntarily. His mouth, with its seductive lower lip, was temptingly close. She couldn't look away.

'You've unlocked my painting again,' Jake whispered, gazing at her lips, a kiss away. His hand searched further, hot on her skin.

She smiled up at him, concentrating hard on not licking her lips.

'Hi, Ashley.'

She jumped a foot. 'Eddie!' she cried out guiltily. 'Hi.'

'Hello.' He nodded coolly, a shuttered expression on his face. Acknowledging Jake, he added, 'I can see you're busy,' and he moved past.

'We'd better get circulating,' she said hastily to Jake, coming back to her senses. 'Not going to sell any of your paintings this way.' What was happening to her? She eyed her empty glass with displeasure and wondered about the strength of the wine on an empty stomach.

'Whatever you say, boss.' He gave her a knowing smile and drifted off.

'Jake, don't drink too much…' she began to say, but he was out of earshot already.

Ashley gazed at Eddie, now on the other side of the room and talking to Zoe, and her heart sank. Of all the people to witness that, it had to be him. Screwing up her eyes in horror, she ran through the guest list in her head; he hadn't been on it. Why was he here? She shouldn't have encouraged Jake; not that he'd needed much. With a twist of her lips, she realised neither had she. 'Oh God,

I need to get laid,' she groaned, to the surprise of the well-dressed woman who had come to stand next to her.

As the evening wore on the crowds thinned. Most, once they'd had their free drinks, disappeared. It left the serious buyers. Going to the desk, Ashley counted up the sales in the book and was pleased to see five paintings had sold already. Writing in the details of a sixth, she looked up. A small crowd had gathered around Jake's portrait of her, from which she could hear raised voices. He'd insisted on it being put in the most prominent position and had flanked it with the sketches done at the riverside. Ashley had avoided it all evening. The painting made her feel uncomfortably exposed.

Drawn by the arguing, she moved nearer and saw the group consisted of Ken's eminent guests, plus Noah, Eddie, Zoe and Ken.

Jake was right in the middle. 'They're not for sale,' he said with an unapologetic shrug.

The woman with the spiky arctic blonde hair, who Ashley had discovered was the gallery owner, Freya Carlisle, laughed. She smoothed down her lime green shift in a disparaging gesture. 'Darling,' she exclaimed. 'You can't display work and refuse to sell it.'

'I created it. I own it. I can do anything I like with it. It's not for sale.' Jake's tone was mulish.

'But whyever not? It's easily the best thing here.'

'I don't have to give a reason.'

'Jake, think about it,' Ken said. 'Freya can give it a much wider audience than we ever could here. I can appreciate you're attached to it, but the whole point of tonight was to get you wider exposure. It's short-sighted to not sell something. And I agree with Freya; it's the best painting here, it deserves to be seen by more people.'

Ashley was aware that Keeley, the reporter from the paper, had nosed in, scenting a story. The last thing Jake needed was to get publicity for being a brat.

He spotted her and pulled her close. Putting an arm around her waist, his hand strayed to her bottom. 'This is the reason I'm not parting with that painting. This is the reason I'm painting again. I've found my muse and I don't intend to part with her or her portrait.' Grabbing her chin, he kissed her hard on the mouth, then waved a hand at the room.

Ashley realised he was drunk. Very drunk.

'You can have the pick of the rest, but leave Ash and her painting alone.'

She disentangled herself, feeling soiled and trying to resist the urge to wipe her mouth. Jake swayed a little at her side.

'Darling boy,' Freya crooned with an underlying malice. 'You're being ridiculous. It's all fine and dandy having a muse, as you so quaintly put it, but the idea of you painting is to *sell* your paintings, including those of your favourite model. Had you forgotten that? Or are you simply dabbling in all this?'

'Let me sort it, Freya,' Ken interrupted. 'Boy's a bit overwrought. I'm sure he'll see sense.'

She gestured to the room. 'Take it from me, Ken, if he doesn't develop a professional attitude, then he's not going to get very far, no matter how wondrous his talent. Despite the common misconception, there really is no room in this world for a diva artist. The days of Brit Art are long over, darling.' She swept off.

The small crowd dispersed, with Ken taking Jake off, probably to talk some sense into him, or at least try to sober him up.

Like a shark nosing for blood, Keeley approached Ashley. 'More intrigue. Your story is getting even more compelling. So, now you're an artist's muse? Extraordinary. You must let me write about you one day.'

'I don't have a story, Keeley,' she replied through clenched teeth. 'There is absolutely no story attached to me. Please forget all about it.'

'Well, you know where I am.' Keeley shrugged. 'Ah,

is that your delightful cousin I spy over there? Do excuse me.'

Ashley went to stand in front of her portrait, hugging her arms to herself. She wished she'd never set eyes on it, wished she'd never agreed to sit for Jake. She revised her opinion of him; while he might be incredibly talented, the man was nothing but trouble.

'It's a beautiful painting,' said Eddie at her side. 'I can see why Jake is reluctant to let it go.'

Ashley remained silent. There was a vibe coming off Eddie which she couldn't work out. Besides, she couldn't trust her answer. 'The artist is risking the next step in his career for the sake of sentimentality,' she said eventually, and on a bitter note. 'We've worked so hard to set all this up for him, and he's throwing it back in our faces.'

'Then he must have an extremely strong attraction to the work, or maybe it's to the sitter?'

She felt Eddie staring at her. Turning to face him, she was taken aback at the flintiness in his eyes.

'Jake and I are friends, or we were. I'm not sure how I'll feel about him after this debacle.'

'Are you sure, Ashley? Are you sure you're friends? Perhaps you should check with him, because we all know the friendship thing gets blurred with you. I thought we were friends and then you jumped my bones.

Maybe Jake is feeling equally confused.' He nodded curtly. 'Goodnight.'

Chapter Twenty-One

'It was such a mess,' Ashley moaned to Petra some days later, as they sat on the edge of the stage during the half-time break at choir. 'There was Jake hanging off me doing spaniel eyes, Keeley nosing in like a terrier after a rat, and Eddie looking like a cross between a wounded puppy and a pit bull.'

'Get you, with the dog analogy.' Petra's brow furrowed. 'Or maybe that's a metaphor?'

'Or maybe you're missing the point? It makes me the bitch in heat.' Ashley sighed. 'The thing is, I was! I haven't missed sex for two years – too busy concentrating on getting better, I suppose. To be honest, it wasn't all that great with Piers, my ex. He was always too busy checking out his reflection and pumping up his biceps.'

'What, while you were doing it?' Petra's eyes went huge.

'Sometimes.' Ashley giggled.

'Nice.'

'Now all I can think about is sex. With *anyone*. I'm not fussy!' Groaning, she hid her burning face in her hands. 'I just want a man. It's all I can think about.' She kicked the stage with her good foot. 'I want a fuuuuuck!' she wailed.

'Oi, potty mouth, and you the teacher too!' Petra giggled. 'Shush now, or you'll frighten everyone. Arthur's looking scared as it is. You'll just have to load up with batteries, girlfriend, unless you jump one of those hot men you've got dangling. Now, I can't provide one – a man, that is – but I can offer you sugar.' She handed over a box. 'Help yourself to a coconut kiss. Not as good as the real thing but the only type of kiss I've got to hand.'

'A what?' Ashley peered in. All she could see were white mounds topped with a glacé cherry. 'They look like breasts with little red nipples.'

Petra huffed. 'Talk about a one-track mind. They're cakes I'm trying out. Biddy insisted it was a favourite recipe of her mum's. Not quite wartime – post-rationing, I think. Bit messy to eat but delish. Have a serviette too. You'll need it.'

Ashley took a cake and held the serviette under it. As she bit into it, coconut showered off. 'Oh my God, it's so sweet it's making my eyes water,' she gasped through a mouthful. 'I can feel my teeth rotting.'

'What can I say? They're mostly condensed milk and egg white. Britain in the fifties must have been on a permanent sugar high.'

'Are you selling them in the café?'

'Yup. The kids love them.'

'I can imagine. Bet their parents don't. Must make them hyper for hours.' Ashley shook her head. 'No thanks, I'll say no to another.'

'Wet wipe?'

'Ooh, yes please.' It came out as a whimper. 'Oh, that's not what you mean.'

Petra roared. 'Girl, you have got to get yourself laid. I meant one of these.' She handed over a wipe from a tub.

'Thanks.' Ashley wiped her fingers. 'And thanks for listening to my frustrated ramblings.'

'No probs,' Petra said cheerfully as she fastened the lid back on the Tupperware box of sticky cakes. 'All mega entertaining.'

'Glad you think so.' Ashley ran her tongue around her mouth, grimacing. 'I'll be picking coconut out of my teeth all during the ABBA medley. Gives me an excuse not to hit the high notes, I suppose. Who would have thought ABBA would be so hard to sing?'

'It's the range required. I might rethink. Been a bit too ambitious.'

'I think most songs are out of Biddy's range.' She winced. 'She just can't sing, can she?'

'Well, to be fair, she is partially deaf. Makes up for it in enthusiasm, though.'

'She certainly does that.' Ashley giggled, thinking back to Biddy's rendition of 'The Wind Beneath My Wings', and then sobered as she remembered that the last time she'd had a similar conversation was with Eddie, in the courtyard, just before they'd kissed with such abandon. Her senses tightened and the energy raced around her body as she remembered how it had felt. It might just be a post-coconut-kiss sugar rush, but she doubted it. Jake was an exciting, sexy man but it was Eddie who had really set her on fire; he was the one who had awakened this burning sexuality in her, this longing.

She looked around at the theatre. Arthur was holding court with Biddy and Beryl and one or two other women. Near the kitchen, a few of the book group members were sipping tea and discussing something heatedly, with Amy trying to placate. Ennis, of allotment fame, and Zoe were sitting chatting at the front with Zoe trying to hide her boredom – and failing. No Eddie. After the first session he'd not returned. She could hardly blame him. He probably had better things to do with his time than drive all the way over to Berecombe for a bit of a singsong. She wondered if he'd had his big meeting with Fizz TV yet and how all that was going. Would she ever see him again? And what would she say to him if she ever did?

'Earth calling Planet Ashley.'

'Mmm?'

'Oh hello, you're back with us. We lost you somewhere for a second. Was it nice?' Petra's voice was fully loaded with sarcasm.

'Was what nice?' Ashley looked around for her water bottle. The coconut kiss had given her a raging thirst.

'Wherever you went?'

Ashley flashed her an apologetic smile. They sat in silence while she gulped down water and then she asked, 'Are you going on the steam train ride and picnic?'

'Yeah! Wouldn't miss it for the world. Do you want to borrow an outfit? I think it's fancy dress. Some of the children from the primary school are coming along too, with their gas mask boxes and labels.'

Ashley looked blank.

'They're going to be "evacuated".' Petra put speech marks around the word with her fingers. 'Did World War

Two as their history topic in the summer term. Coming along in all their 1939 finery.'

'In that case, yes, I'd like to borrow something. You know,' Ashley said slowly, 'what we should do is sing a few songs.'

'We're about to, you know, when everyone comes back from their break,' Petra said, as if explaining to the hard of understanding. 'Not sure I'm ever going to feed you sugar again.'

'No, I mean *on the train*. Some World War Two songs. I bet the children learned a few as part of their project. Fun ones as well as "The White Cliffs of Dover". And there's bound to be quite a few choir members on board too.'

'Honor would be cool with it. She teaches at Berecombe Primary and pops into the café all the time, that's how I found out her class are being evacuated. She's always up for a laugh. We could sing "Run Rabbit Run". Maybe "We're Going to Hang out the Washing".' Petra clapped her hands together excitedly, putting the box of coconut kisses in peril. 'The kids are Year Four, they'll love it!'

'It would be fun. I'm sure the evacuees at the time sang to keep their spirits up.'

'I bet they did. We can start on "Run Rabbit Run" after the break. It's fairly simple. Thanks, Ash. It's a great idea.' Petra looked around the theatre, nearly ready to call the choir back. 'Shame we've no Eddie and Noah tonight. We're a bit short on men.'

'Noah's in a meeting and sends his apologies, but Eddie might be my fault. I still haven't cleared things up between us. He didn't exactly storm out after our conversation at Jake's exhibition, but it came close.'

'He's jealous, girl. You did say you were a bitch in heat. With all the boy doggies panting after you.'

Ashley grimaced. She was regretting the dog imagery. 'I don't know about that. Eddie said he just wants to be friends.'

'Except he didn't say that, Ash, girl. He's *settling* for that. He wants more from you. He's bound to be jealous when he sees you with another man, especially one as lush as our charismatic resident painter. Are you and Jake getting it on then?'

'In a manner of speaking.' Ashley caught the gleam in Petra's eyes. 'But not like that. We're friends. Can't say I wasn't tempted at one point, but decided it would be safer to be friends.'

Petra rolled her eyes. 'Another friend. Thought you were after a shag.'

'Yes, *friends*,' Ashley emphasised. 'We've got that art connection and he's good painting company.'

'But he wants more too.' Petra nudged her elbow suggestively.

'He's hinted. He was drunk at the exhibition, though. I don't think he knew what he was doing that night.'

'In vino verity and all that,' Petra misquoted. 'Come off it, Ashley, he fancies his rocks off you. How do you feel about him?'

Ashley thought back to how Jake had looked at her from his smouldering blue eyes. 'As I said, I was tempted for a moment but he's younger than me,' she began.

'Not a problem.'

'It's not just that, though. He's at a different stage in his life. His is just beginning.'

'Oh, for fuck's sake Ash, you're hardly at the Zimmer frame stage yet, woman!'

Ashley winced. Petra was losing patience with her. 'It's not his age, it's his ambitions. We want very different things.' She sighed. 'I mean, I'm ready to settle down, maybe, if the right man comes along. Have children. If I can.' She shot a look at Petra; they'd only lightly discussed the after-effects of the accident. 'And that's a whole other Pandora's Box. Most importantly, I'm ready to find some roots. In Berecombe possibly. Jake will be off somewhere as soon as his big commission comes in, which it will, despite his atrocious behaviour the other night.'

'Great for a quick shag, though. Before he goes. Get it out of the system.'

Ashley laughed. 'As a matter of fact, he said something very similar, but you know that's not my style. I just can't do the one-night-stand thing, never have. I can't believe I was even thinking about it, I wasn't in my right mind. It must have been his star appeal.' She paused. 'I want someone who will be a great dad and who will be around. Jake's too flaky.'

'Whereas Eddie is desperate to have kids, is as steady as a rock—'

'And having a baby with his ex,' Ashley shot back.

Petra groaned. 'When are you going to let that go?' she said tersely. 'At his age, he could easily have an ex-wife and three children tucked away.'

'You know, Petra, that might have been easier to deal with. I just can't get past it. All I can see is him with Bree and the baby.' Ashley felt ridiculous tears prickle. 'If only it was different.'

'But it isn't, girlfriend. If you want my opinion, I think you're mad to let this man go. And by this man, I mean Eddie. I think he's exactly what you're looking for. What you need.' Petra put a hand on Ashley's. 'For God's sake, not that I believe in Him, why don't you try to talk to him about it? Explain how it's making you feel.'

'How can I, Petra? I don't even know myself. It's all so complicated.' Ashley heard the whine of self-pity in her voice but couldn't stop it. She was beginning to irritate herself. It seemed she wasn't alone.

'Well, you know what,' Petra snapped, in a curiously hard voice. 'Life fucking is. Maybe you should get used to that fact.' She slid off the stage, leaving Ashley staring at her retreating back and wondering where the flare of temper had come from.

Chapter Twenty-Two

'Well, don't you all look a picture!' said Ruby as she greeted Petra, Noah and Ashley as they rushed onto the station platform.

She and Biddy were standing by the open door of a magnificent Pullman carriage – brass, chrome and black paint glossy in the sunshine. From the engine at the front smoke drifted up into the turquoise sky and made the air thick with the smell of hot coal. Ashley thought the train looked alive, like a great dragon impatiently waiting to roar and fly. Over a quiet hissing she could hear the excited yells of children on board. Everybody else must be on the train. They'd had a fraught drive to Berecombe Junction, having been caught in the tailback from an accident. The station, although the one which pre-Beeching had served the town, was some way out and off the busy A35. They'd only just made it. Her nerves were in shreds and she'd tried hard not to panic and flashback when they'd driven past the crumpled wreckage of the cars involved.

'Give us a whirl so I can see you properly,' Ruby insisted.

Each obliged, Petra holding out the skirts of her tea dress, Noah doffing his straw Panama with aplomb and Ashley shakily turning round so Ruby could better see her pink dress with the ditzy print. Petra had loaned her the outfit and it came complete with a neat little Robin Hood hat and matching gloves in red. With her hair up in a victory roll and the hat perched at an impossible angle over the top, Ashley had never felt more ladylike.

'Shame we couldn't have managed all this for VE Day, as originally planned,' Biddy put in tartly.

'What can I say except to apologise,' Noah answered. 'Apparently, they were all booked up until now and, as we wanted to charter the entire train, it was rather tricky to find a date free. Still, we can celebrate VE Day today, just a little later than we'd hoped.'

'Two months later,' Biddy grumbled.

'But we've splendid weather for it,' Noah said, channelling a charming 1940s movie star with ease. 'And rather nicer than the rain I seem to remember we had on the eighth of May. Maybe,' he said with a twinkle in his eye, 'it was meant to be? A picnic lunch will be so much more pleasant in the sunshine. Shall we board the train, ladies? It's about to depart.'

'Ooh, you sound just like Ronald Colman,' Ruby cackled as she took his arm.

Ashley waited until the others had boarded The Berecombe Belle, watching as they found their seats. On top of the shock at seeing the accident, she was nervous about today. The recent awkwardness which had developed between her and Petra had cast a cloud over what ought to be a fun day. She'd liked the woman almost as soon as they had met, admired her singing talent and loved her 'Let's tackle it head on' approach to life, but ever since their weird spat at choir, things hadn't been quite the same. Petra had been offhand when handing over the outfit for today, no giggles or naughty gossiping, and Ashley couldn't work out why. The smashed-up cars forced themselves back into her vision. Her breathing was getting out of control and she tried to calm herself. She hoped everyone was okay; there had been two ambulances and a police car attending.

Biddy turned to her just before she went to haul herself up the steps of the carriage. 'Stop sparrow catching, lass.' She peered closer. 'You all right? Not afraid of an old steam train, are you?' She batted something away, tutting. 'They might look impressive, but you always forget the smoke smuts. Just as well I remembered not to wear white.'

A great belch of snarling and hissing came from The Belle's engine, making Ashley jump violently.

Biddy laughed. 'You forget that and all. Give me a diesel any day. Less romantic, I grant you, but not so alarming. Come on, girl, stir your stumps, we've got to get evacuated.'

Nerves still raw, Ashley followed her onto the train, trying not to trip in her hurry. She paused for a second, hearing the guard slamming doors, making his way systematically from the rear. It was dim inside compared with the glaring July sunshine, and as she waited for her eyes to adjust she was greeted by Beryl.

'Ashley, my lovely, I've saved you a seat right here. Come along, hurry up and sit yourself down before the train starts. You don't want to be standing when it moves off.'

She perched on the edge of the seat Beryl pointed out, closed her eyes and did her breathing exercises, feeling her heartbeat slow. The guard let rip a piercing whistle and immediately the beast of a train gathered its energy before shuddering and chugging slowly out of the station. From a carriage further down the train she heard the children give an enormous cheer and smiled, feeling calmer. There was definitely something endearing about a steam train.

'This is pretty cool, isn't it?' said a familiar American voice opposite.

Ashley felt her cheeks burn. Opening her eyes and taking off her sunglasses, she said, 'Hello, Eddie.' Her heart leaped into an irregular rhythm again.

The carriage was set up with single seats facing one another over a tiny table with a pretty tablecloth and next to a window. On the opposite side, Beryl was chatting animatedly to Biddy, and Noah and Petra were presumably somewhere further down with Ruby. Although there was more room than on a modern train, Eddie still seemed too big for the space; his legs were bent up uncomfortably. Biting her lip, she studied him. He wore a cream linen suit and, while not very in keeping with the period, looked good enough to eat. She squashed the thought down. Thinking like that had got her into a whole heap of trouble.

It seemed an age since she'd seen him, but Jake's exhibition had only been the month before. She stayed silent, not knowing what to say, and cursed Biddy and Beryl, whom she strongly suspected of plotting to make this meeting happen. They were probably in cahoots with Ruby and Noah. Summoning every last scrap of calm, she added, 'I didn't know you were coming today.' It sounded lame even to her ears.

'Thought I would. Thought I'd celebrate.'

'What, VE Day?'

'Well, that as well, but it's July fourth.'

'Oh, I see.' Ashley relaxed a little. Eddie seemed more amenable than when they'd last met. With another blush she remembered she'd had Jake's hand down the front of her dress and had been on the brink of snogging him at the time. Trying not to wince, she realised what a mistake Jake had been and vowed to make more effort with Eddie. Maybe Petra was right? It was time to be a grown-up about all of this.

'What do you usually do to celebrate? At home, I mean.'

'I go back to Mom and Dad's in Rockport. Shove a few steaks on the barbecue, have a beer or two. Watch the parade on TV. Usually end up sitting on the front porch putting the world to rights while Dad smokes the one cigar a year Mom lets him have.'

Ashley smiled. 'Sounds lovely.'

'Yeah. It's a good excuse to catch up. I'm looking forward to seeing them again in September.'

'September?' Ashley's heart flipped painfully.

Eddie eyed her speculatively. 'Going back for the birth of the baby.'

'Oh yes. Of course.' Of course he'd want to be there for the birth of his child.

'It's a boy, did I tell you?'

'No.' It came out as a strangled whisper. Ashley added, with immense effort, 'That's lovely. You must be pleased.' She couldn't imagine anything much cuter than a miniature version of Eddie. She could see him now, a sturdy toddler with blond hair and chubby star-shaped hands. Something deep inside her contracted painfully.

'Boy or girl, I wouldn't have minded either way.'

Ashley gulped and ploughed on. 'Have you thought of any names?'

'Bree's got a few in mind, but I'm trying to persuade her to wait to see what the little fella looks like before we decide.'

It sounded as if he was involved with the baby, but then, what did she expect? He desperately wanted it. And being the man he was, he would offer Bree all the support he could. Swallowing tears, she asked, 'Are your parents pleased?'

'Sure. First grandkid.' His mouth twisted. 'Guess it could have happened another way, but Mom will still dote on him.'

'And I remember you saying she's close to Bree?'

'They're good friends, yeah.'

There was a pause while they were served coffee and

shortbread biscuits. It was all very elegantly done, with a silver pot and tiny cups. It gave Ashley much-needed time to pull herself together. *Be the grown-up,* she intoned silently.

'Shall I?' he offered. 'Pass the creamer, will you? Oh, you don't call it that over here, do you?'

'Milk jug,' Ashley supplied. She pulled a face, quite pleased at how she was handling all this. 'Bit more prosaic.'

He poured coffee, grinning. 'You say *potato*, I say *patata*. You say *tomato*, I say *tamata*.'

'Let's call the whole thing off,' she finished… and then sank into silence, appalled at what she'd said.

'Is that what you want to do, Ashley?' he asked levelly. 'Call the whole thing off?'

She lifted the cup with fingers that only slightly trembled and sipped the coffee. It was good. Hot and strong and just what she needed. 'Is there anything to call off?'

'I don't know. You tell me.'

'We've… we've tried being friends.' She looked down, unable to meet his eyes. 'I have to apologise for my behaviour that time at choir. I don't know what came over me.'

'No need to apologise, Ash, although you've had me guessing these past few months.'

'I,' she gulped, 'I find you very attractive.'

'That's good to hear.' He grinned as she finally made eye contact. 'And you know I find you equally so. I'm not sure that's the problem between us, though, is it?'

'No.' It came out on a strangled whisper. 'And the friends thing didn't work out very well.'

He frowned. 'Not too well, no. Somehow I don't think we're capable of being friends. Or not *just* friends, that is.' Before she had a chance to answer, he added abruptly, 'Ash, can I ask you something?'

'Of course.'

'This guy, Jack.'

'Jake.'

'Yes, Jake, the painter guy. How close are you two?'

'We're friends.' She caught his cynical expression. 'No really, we are just friends. We like to paint together sometimes. I'm hoping he hasn't blown his chances and there'll be a gallery offering him space, or better still, a high-profile commission. He'll head out of Berecombe and off to the bright lights as soon as that happens. And quite rightly so.'

Eddie cleared his throat. 'It's just that you two looked pretty cosy that night at his exhibition.'

Ashley felt herself blush. 'Erm…'

'My turn to apologise. I'm sorry. I couldn't handle seeing you together. I was plain jealous, is all.'

She expelled a breath, a little light-headed at the idea of Eddie being jealous. 'I will admit to going a bit crazy that night. Maybe it was the relief that it was going well after all the hard work of organising it, or maybe it was that I'd had too much to drink on an empty stomach. You know, under all the bluster, the starry ego, the outrageous and compulsive flirting, he's a nice bloke with a lot of talent, just maybe not the maturity to handle it right now. I can assure you Jake and I are just friends. Nothing more.' She tugged her gloves off, nervous. 'Why do you ask? Why do you want to know, Eddie?'

The train jolted, making the cups and saucers rattle and the pink curtain tassels thump against the window. It all sounded overly loud and echoed the frantic beating of her heart.

'I saw him. In Exeter.'

'Okay,' Ashley said slowly, deflated. Where was all this was going? It wasn't the answer she'd yearned for. Her throat ached. If he were to declare his feelings again, would she have the courage to give him the answer he wanted? She simply didn't know. Or, after her recent behaviour, the right. All she knew was, she longed for him.

'He was with Zoe. From the body language,' Eddie shrugged, 'and the fact he had his tongue down her throat, I guessed *they* were more than friends.'

'Oh.' It came out on a long, drawn-out breath.

Eddie pulled a face. 'See? I knew you had feelings for him. Jeez, I've been tearing myself inside out about what to tell you. Whether to tell you.'

'I'm concerned about Zoe. She's too young to get mixed up with someone like Jake. I'm worried she'll get hurt.'

'Once a teacher, always a teacher.'

'Yes, I suppose so. I really like the girl. I don't want her heart broken.'

'She's technically an adult. She can probably look after herself.'

'Yes, possibly.' Ashley wondered if Zoe was as tough as she liked to appear.

'So, what are you going to do?'

'What would you do if, at twenty, you were told your boyfriend was an incorrigible flirt with no morals?'

'Well, firstly I'd question my interest in this boyfriend, as I'm most definitely straight.'

Ashley managed a laugh. 'And then?'

'And then I'd ignore what I'd been told and go my own sweet way. Which is precisely what happened.'

'When people warned you about Bree, you mean?'

'Yup. Took no notice and carried on that self-destructive path. And look how that turned out.'

'But you'll have your baby, your son,' she said quietly.

'Yes, I'll have him, but at what cost, Ash? Is it going to mean losing out on the chance to be with you? What does our future look like, now that we know he'll always be in my life?' He leaned forward and took her hand. 'Can there even be a future for us? Ashley, do you think we could start over?'

And at that precise moment, as Ashley opened her mouth and tried to form an answer, the train went into a tunnel.

Chapter Twenty-Three

The world went black; there was a sort of sucking sensation on her ears and the train noise was deafening. The Belle's whistle hooted long and strident and Ashley heard frightened squeals from the children. Biddy, sitting opposite, cried out loudly, 'What the ruddy Nora?' and then they were clear of the tunnel and blinking in the light.

'Still here,' Eddie said.

'Yes, still here. Eddie, I—' she began but got no further.

Petra appeared. 'You coming to join the choir, Ash? We're all going into the next carriage to join the kids and sing a few songs. Although this is confusing the hell out of their history learning. Half of them think it's VE Day and can't understand why they're getting evacuated when the war's over.'

Ashley swore, maddened by the woman's bad-tempered interruption. She began to get up, but the train rocked and shuddered and she nearly lost her balance.

'Here, let me. I'll help.' Eddie rose. 'Is it far to the next carriage?' he asked Petra.

She shrugged. 'Through the connecting thingy. Well, come on then, what are you waiting for?' She turned on her heel and marched off.

'Thank you,' Ashley answered, sarcasm dripping. She'd left her stick at home, thinking it ruined the look of her gorgeous outfit, and the thought of walking along on a bucking train made her panic levels rise again. Really, why was Petra still being so horrible? She could have stayed to help. 'I'm sure I'll manage on my own,' she added sharply to the woman's retreating back.

Eddie misunderstood. He recoiled, thinking she was addressing him. 'It's okay. I want to come. I'd like to hear the children sing. You go first and I'll be behind.' He held up his hands in surrender. 'Promise I won't lay a finger on you unless you fall.'

Shit. He'd taken her dismissive tone at face value. She groaned inwardly. This was getting farcical. If only they could be alone and talk. Then she could explain why this was all so complicated. Grasping each seat as she inched her way along, she found it wasn't as difficult as she'd feared. That was, until she got to the passage connecting the two carriages. Wrenching open the door, she was blasted by noise from the wheels and a frantic rush of wind. Eddie came up behind and put his hands under her shoulders to steady her. Despite the bliss of his touch, she was relieved to get through the horrible rubber, accordion-like tunnel, which shifted beneath her feet, and to where the school children were.

This carriage had a long corridor down one side, with compartments going off on the right. It was straight out of an Agatha Christie film and, from the noise, it sounded as if someone was being murdered too.

She and Eddie could get no further along the corridor as the choir members had filled it. Eddie looked around and located a flip-down seat, which Ashley sank onto gratefully. She was all for trying new things, but this might have been an adventure one wobbly step too far in her recuperation. It was the motion of the train that was making things so difficult. On firm, level ground she sometimes forgot she was still healing. The moving train was putting her balance out.

The screeches and squeals from the excited children were too much and she felt her leg muscles tense painfully as she tried to stay on the slippery seat. With the wind from the open windows buffeting the carriage, Ashley was beginning to regret coming. Then, from somewhere halfway down the carriage, came the sound of hands clapping together. A voice boomed out – it could only be Biddy – yelling at everyone to be quiet. Another, younger, voice sounded. It must belong to the class teacher.

'Are we ready, everyone? Remember, we've sung this one in school. *Clang clang clang goes the trolley...*'

At first Ashley was too uncomfortable to join in, but the singing was infectious and the children's enjoyment so innocently cheerful that she gradually forgot to be embarrassed. By the time they'd got to 'Run Rabbit Run' she was singing with gusto. A rendition of 'Mairzy Doats' finished it all off, with the children shouting out the nonsense lyrics and falling about with laughter.

Then there came a great wheezing, the brakes hissed and the train began to slow. They must be reaching their destination. As Ashley began to get up, Eddie put his hand on her shoulder. 'Why not wait until we've completely stopped? It'll be easier to get back to our seats when it's stationary. Or you can even get off onto the platform and get back on further along the train. It's not going anywhere until we head back to Berecombe.'

Ashley sat again, grateful for his thoughtfulness. They waited until the choir had emptied from the corridor before following in their wake. Eddie was right.

The Great Summer Street Party Part 2

It was much easier navigating the connecting passageway when the train was still. As they were collecting their things, they were startled to hear some kind of trumpet blast out a shrill impression of The Belle's whistle.

'Hey, get a load of this.' Eddie ducked his head to look out of the window.

Ashley peered over his shoulder. There was, of all things, a 1940s-style big band playing on the platform to welcome them. Having been started off by the trumpet, the band launched into a lively rendition of 'Chattanooga Choo Choo'. Ashley recognised it from singing it at choir. Noah was steering two GI veterans and Ruby to some seats in the middle of the platform, facing the band. Teacher Honor Miles was shepherding her pupils into position and the choir members were being arranged by Petra on the other flank of the guests of honour. The other passengers stood at one end looking on with bemusement.

'Guess we'd better get off and join in the fun.' Eddie held out a hand. Ashley took it, climbed down from the train on slightly wobbly legs and made her way to the choir.

'Come on, ladies,' Petra called. 'We know this one. It's one of our favourites.' She nodded to the leader of the band and the introduction to 'Boogie Woogie Bugle Boy' blasted out.

Ashley loved this one. She always suspected choir members were secretly channelling the Andrews Sisters or Christina Aguilera, depending on the generation to which they belonged, when singing it. Class Four had obviously learned it too, as they joined in with gusto. They looked very sweet, the boys in shorts and blazers and the girls in pretty dresses and cardigans. Everyone carried a brown cardboard box for their gas mask and wore a poignant label bearing their name and school. Ashley had a lump in her throat, making singing impossible. It was a lovely sunny day full of fun and escapism but, for the children who'd really had to be evacuated, it must have been a mixed adventure. She could only imagine the jumble of excitement and fear they must have felt; leaving all that they knew and loved to be taken halfway around the country to live with strangers. She would have hated it.

Ruby, however, who had experienced evacuation for real, showed no sign of introspection. She had an enormous smile on her face and was clapping along to the singing. Noah had snaffled the Nikon from Ashley and was taking copious amounts of photographs and trying not to get in the way. Then Ashley noticed Chloe

Deverell directing a cameraman; she was surprised *Focus Southwest* was covering the event.

Petra, having got the singing going, turned her back on the choir and was joined by the other members of The Jenny WRENs. Another surprise. The band played louder, as if in appreciation of the girls' trademark dance moves: hands coyly at their sides, knees bent, bottoms swaying seductively.

With sandbags piled up against one wall, a vintage cart with its heavy horse tethered in the lane, the station master dressed up in a period uniform and posters declaring *Buy Defence Bonds* and *Careless Talk Costs Lives!* decorating the station, it was as if they had left the twenty-first century behind them at Berecombe Junction.

After 'There'll be Bluebirds Over the White Cliffs of Dover' the singing was rounded off by The Belle joining in the fun and letting out an ear-ripping screech of a train whistle.

'Well, wasn't that wonderful?' Beryl declared when it was all over. 'And didn't the children do marvellously? Time for lunch now, don't you think? Arthur's bringing ours up by car. Saves carrying it. Apparently, there's a picnic area over the lane. Benches too, so we oldies don't have to sit on the grass.' She chuckled. 'It's not the sitting down that's the problem, of course – it's the getting up!'

Ashley smiled at her; she was immensely fond of

Beryl. 'Then we'd better go and grab a good spot.' Looking around, she realised someone was missing. 'Have you seen Eddie? I can't see him.'

'No, my lovely, I haven't, and he's an easy one to spot. Wasn't he singing with the choir?'

Ashley shook her head. 'I lost him in the crowd.'

'Maybe he'll catch up with us at the picnic?' Beryl suggested.

'Yes, probably.' Ashley couldn't see him anywhere; she was still worried he'd taken her curt response on the train as her answer to his question about their future. Frowning, she thought over what she'd said about Jake; had she made it clear enough they were just friends? Frustratingly, the conversation had got side-lined by discussing Zoe and Bree.

She bumped into a Class Four parent helper and apologised. Making her way carefully through the children who had now, *en masse*, decided they were desperate for the loo, she was grateful she'd never been tempted into primary school teaching. She couldn't see Eddie anywhere. Sending a sympathetic smile to Honor, who was directing the parent helpers while simultaneously dealing with a little boy's nosebleed, she asked, 'Can I help in any way? I'm secondary trained but willing to wade in.'

'Oh, bless you, but we're fine, thank you. It looks

more chaotic than it actually is.' Honor peered at the boy. 'All finished now, Amrit? Take it easy for the next half hour. No racing around, you hear?' Addressing Ashley, she said, 'Once we get them all sat down with their sandwiches, peace will reign. For a while anyway. They got a bit excited by the train whistle. Lots of Hogwarts fans in the class. Thanks for the offer, though. You go and enjoy your day, unencumbered by thirty nine-year-olds!'

Biddy and Ruby had found a bench and table a little way apart from the crowds and waved at Beryl and Ashley to join them.

'Arthur's dropped off a veritable feast,' Biddy said. 'Including,' she paused and then flourished a bottle of champagne, 'this! I thought, seeing as we're about to enter a World War, or celebrate the end of one – I've got mightily confused about what today is all about and, to be frank, I don't much care – we'd do it in style!' she said cheerfully. As she eased the cork out, she added, 'And I've a message for you, Ashley. Your Eddie sends his apologies. He can't join us, as he's had to go back to town. He begged a lift off Arthur.'

Chapter Twenty-Four

The picnic was delightful. Biddy unpacked, along with the champagne, tiny quails' eggs, smoked salmon and cream cheese bagels and strawberries. A breeze tempered the heat and it was almost the perfect day. Almost. To make it perfect, it needed Eddie. As she tried to eat, Ashley wondered why he'd gone and hoped it wasn't anything she'd said. Surely he didn't really think she had feelings for Jake?

'I'll have to go and powder my nose,' Ruby said when they'd finished. 'Although I've eaten that much, I'm not sure I can move. Biddy, that was a feast. Thank you.'

'I'll come with you,' Beryl said and then groaned as she tried to move. 'But can we take it slowly?'

They staggered off, crossing the lane and going back into the station. Ashley watched them with affection.

'Ruby's right. That was wonderful food. Thank you for letting me share. It made my ham and mustard sandwiches look a bit pathetic.' She noticed, for the first time, Biddy was without the faithful poodle. 'No Elvis today? He would have enjoyed the picnic too.'

'Thought it best he stayed at home. Bit too much commotion going on, on a day like today. Thought he might distract the kiddies, too. That teacher's got enough on her plate.'

'True.'

'He's at home with Arthur and his Daisy. That's his retriever. Getting on a bit now, the love.' Biddy blinked rapidly, looking close to tears. 'That's the trouble with dogs. As soon as you get one you know you'll probably have to say goodbye one day.' She cleared her throat, embarrassed at the show of emotion.

'I hadn't thought about that before. You must be devoted to Elvis. I mean, he's not just a pet, he's your helper too.'

'Wouldn't be without him. He's seven now but poodles go on for a good while.'

'Will he ever retire? Or is he an assistance dog for life?'

Biddy sniffed. 'They make them retire at eleven but he won't be going anywhere. Got a home for life, has Elvis.' She peered into her plastic champagne flute and drained the dregs. 'That reminds me, I've got a problem.' A certain cunning replaced the affection in her voice.

Ashley stiffened. 'What's that?'

'I've a friend who has to go into a nursing home. The same one Jimmy Larcombe was in, as it happens, so I know she'll be looked after.'

'Then what's the problem?'

'It's her deaf-assistance dog. She can't go with her.'

'Oh, that's so sad. And cruel!'

Biddy shrugged. 'It's the way it is. They have to have rules in these places. Other folk in there might be scared of dogs, or be allergic.'

'True.'

'It's just that if I can find her a home, somewhere local, Janet can see her dog every now and again, and know the little thing is happy and cared for.'

Ashley frowned. 'Won't the charity or organisation, or whatever it is that runs these things, get it rehomed, or give it to another person in need?'

'Bronte's coming up for nine. Too late to get her settled into another working home and get her adjusted to a new person's needs.'

'Bronte. Pretty name.' Too late, Ashley felt herself being sucked in.

'She's a pretty little dog. Black poodle, same as Elvis. Same parents, in fact. Gentle little girl, she is.'

'Why don't you take her on?'

'Can't, not with Daisy. She's on her last legs and grumpy with it. Don't think it's fair to land her with another dog in the house.'

'Poor Bronte.' Ashley's heart softened. 'What will happen to her?' She batted a wasp away, thoughtfully.

'I thought maybe you'd like her.'

'Biddy!' she laughed. 'I can't have a dog.'

'Does your letting contract say so?'

'No, but—'

'Then what's the problem? Do you good. Get you out and about. Dogs always need a walk.'

'I've never had a dog. I wouldn't have the first idea what to do with it.'

'Her.'

'Her.'

'Not a lot you have to do. Love, food and exercise. Dogs are very simple.' Biddy huffed. 'Lot simpler than people.'

'But there's work. I work at the Arts Workshop now.'

'Bronte's an assistance dog. She's trained to go anywhere. She'd sit at your feet and wouldn't make a murmur.'

A picture began to form in Ashley's head of Bronte in a cosy bed in her tiny office at work. Ken wouldn't mind, surely?

'And nothing loves you like a poodle does. They're clever little buggers. Soon learn to read your moods.'

The picture changed to the sofa in the flat and a little furry body cuddled up next to her. She'd been lonely since Petra had cooled. A dog would be company.

'She'd come fully house trained.'

'That's a relief. I wouldn't have a clue.'

'They pick it up quickly, do poodles. As I say, they're bright doggies. And don't shed hair either.'

'Another bonus.' Ashley shook her head, coming back to her senses. 'Sorry, Biddy, the whole thing's ridiculous. I can't have a dog.'

'Why not? Going somewhere? Thought you were settling in Berecombe. Putting down roots.'

'I am, but—'

'But nothing,' Biddy said briskly, turning her champagne flute upside down and trapping the persistent wasp. 'You're ideal for one another. Come along to meet Janet and Bronte, and see how you feel then, lass. Don't have to make a decision until you meet her.'

'But what if I have to go away?'

'Like where?'

Ashley was about to say to meetings and courses but realised all those belonged to another life. Pre the demarcation line that the accident had drawn. 'To my parents,' she said, flailing for a response. 'My mum's not keen on dogs, says they're dirty.' She had a brainwave. 'What if I have to go to a hospital appointment?'

'Not a problem. I'd be happy to have Bronte for a bit. Or house sit. Think about it. Come and meet her and then decide. And don't worry about her age, young Ashley. Poodles have been known to go on to seventeen or so.' Biddy began to collect the picnic stuff as if to say, *There, that's sorted, another problem solved.* 'I'll leave these things here and pop to the loo, if you don't mind.'

Ashley watched her stride purposefully over the field and disappear. A dog! Could she really adopt a dog? If she was honest with herself, she'd admit she was excited at the prospect. It could work as long as she cleared it with Noah, his landlords, and Ken at work. She'd always badgered her parents for a puppy, like most children, but her mother had always refused, saying they were messy and too much work. Ashley could see her point. But a poodle was tiny and didn't shed. How much mess could one small dog make? She was fond of Elvis, loved how he appeared to dance on his toes, loved his merry little blackcurrants of eyes. He was clever, and placid too – he had to be, to live with Biddy. If Bronte was half as nice a dog, it could work.

She watched as the school children, having scoffed their lunch, were now running off some steam on the far side of the field. There was a complicated-looking game of tag going on and a few of the girls were sitting at the side making daisy chains. Ashley's insides twisted in that familiar, painful way. It was entirely possible that she'd never have children, not from her own body anyway. A dog would be something to love. Something of her own. She thought of Eddie. Biddy was right; in a lot of ways dogs were a whole lot simpler to love than people.

She looked up, eyes squinting against the bright sunlight as Noah came up to her.

'I think it's gone rather well, don't you?' he said. 'Had a good day?'

'I have. And, I don't know how to put this, but I think I may have agreed to adopt a dog.'

Chapter Twenty-Five

'She's a little darling, isn't she?' Noah said as he played tug of war with Bronte on the floor of the flat three weeks later. Like most females, the dog had been quickly won over by his charm.

'She is.' Ashley regarded the black fluff-ball with affection. 'I'm so glad I agreed to take her.'

'Did you have much choice where Biddy was concerned?'

'No.' Ashley laughed. 'Although, weirdly, the woman seems to know my needs better than I do. And I wouldn't have dreamed of adopting her if the Dimmocks hadn't approved.'

'They're a great couple,' Noah said of his landlords. 'Besides, I'm not sure they could refuse, seeing as this used to be a dog-friendly holiday let.'

'Even so, I don't want to put my home into jeopardy. I like it here. The flat suits me and I love living in Berecombe.'

'What's not to like? Oh,' he said to Bronte, as she rolled over, 'it's tummy rub time now, is it?' Looking up, he asked, 'How did my sainted Aunty Ann take it?'

'I'll give you three guesses.'

'Ouch. Does this mean you're out of the will and I inherit?'

'Most probably. She's spitting feathers. Dad, on the other hand, thinks it's hilarious. Claims he's never seen me as a dog person, particularly not one with a, and I quote, "poofy poodle".'

'Nothing poofy about our Bronte,' Noah defended stoutly. 'One of the most intelligent dog breeds.' At this, Bronte thrust her bottom up in the air and sat on her head.

'You might need to rethink that.' Ashley giggled. She was so glad she'd agreed to take Bronte in. There had been one or two teething problems as the dog had adapted, but she had brought much-needed joy and companionship. Ashley wouldn't be without her.

'When are you going to take her to visit Janet?'

'Biddy advised leaving it a while, to give them both a chance to get settled.'

'Sounds sensible. It's a shame you didn't have her for

the train ride. I bet Bronte would have loved that. It's also a shame Eddie had to leave with Arthur.'

'Yes.' Ashley fell silent for a moment. 'I heard he'd been called into a meeting. To do with this TV show he's doing?'

'Yes, they're nearly ready to begin filming. Using some studios up in Bristol, apparently, but there'll be quite a lot of location work involved too. The first series is going to feature the southwest and then, if it's popular, they'll look at other regions.'

'He'll be away a lot, then.' As time went on, it seemed to Ashley as if she was losing Eddie; even the tentative and troubled connection between them was weakening. What with that and Petra's strange attitude, she was beginning to rely more and more on Bronte for company. 'How will that impact his university teaching?'

'He was trying to decide whether or not to leave, or at least cut down his hours. He was waiting to see how the new telly job was going to work out.'

How little she knew about him these days. How little they'd talked on the train. And then the day's events had overtaken them and the moment had been snatched away. She had the horrible feeling she'd stupidly missed her chance for something wonderful with him. Her heart squeezed in pain. How could she put this right and take him up on his offer of starting over? But would she ever see him again? He was probably off filming somewhere or maybe had even returned to the States. Choking down sudden tears, she said, 'I'm sure he'll be a huge hit, whatever he does. He's always struck me as someone who is naturally successful at anything he attempts. Maybe it's all that uber-confidence.'

Noah gave a short laugh. 'He's not so hot on the old relationship front though, is he? This mess he's got himself involved in with Bree is really something.'

'He couldn't just abandon her though, could he? Not when she's having his baby. He's too honourable a man for that.'

'Uh-oh, am I finally detecting a sea change here, coz? Sounds very much like you're defending him.'

Ashley clicked her fingers at Bronte and the dog obligingly jumped up on the sofa for a cuddle. She teased her woolly ears gently. 'If Ella had had a baby,' she said, referring to his most recent ex, 'and you knew it was yours, what would you do?'

'Give her the support she wanted.' The reply was immediate. 'Help raise my child.'

'Of course you would, because that's the sort of man you are. But how do you think it would impact on your relationship with Petra?'

'Not sure I have a relationship with Petra. She's been a slippery soul recently.'

'Agreed. There's something going on with her, isn't there? I've tried talking to her, but she keeps batting me off. But what if you and she were getting serious, into something that had the potential to be for life, and she wasn't happy about the baby situation?'

Noah blew out a breath. 'Oh, I don't know, Ash. We're all different people. One thing I'd make sure of is that I kept the channels of communication open.'

'Which I haven't.'

'Which you most definitely haven't.'

'Yes, all right,' she said irritably. 'Things got in the way.'

'Things, or a certain artist by the name of Jake Tremayne?'

'There was nothing between me and Jake.'

'Trouble is, it didn't look that way to everyone else – Eddie included.'

Ashley's face flamed. She hugged Bronte to her. God, she'd been stupid about Jake. She wondered how Zoe was getting on. Jake had left Berecombe the previous week, a commission finally coming through. An oil company wanted a portrait of its CEO and was willing to pay well. It meant Jake was set on the first rung of his career. As the CEO was a woman, Ashley could guess how that would pan out. It was a relief that the man was no longer around to complicate things.

Noah clambered to his feet and switched on the kettle. 'Eddie asked if I could give him your mobile number. Can't believe you haven't swapped them before. He asked as he thought you were still, to use his words, "pissed at him when you talked on the train".' He swung round, scrubbing a mug dry with a tea-towel. 'Are you telling me you didn't sort things out? Didn't tell him how things with Bree make you feel and, most importantly, why?'

Ashley shook her head. 'Didn't really have a chance. Petra came and got us to sing with the children, and then he had to leave with Arthur to get to his meeting. He's a busy man these days. Remember you said Petra was being slippery? Well, so is Eddie, but in a different way. I don't think he has time for me now.'

'Well, he's going through some things.' Noah warmed the pot; he knew she liked tea made properly. 'I know you said he's mustard keen on having kids, but I wouldn't have thought this was the way he saw it happening. His child will be in the States, and meanwhile his career is really taking off over here. Can't be easy for him.'

'It's not easy for anyone.'

He rolled his eyes. 'Which is why you need to talk. Can I pass on your number?'

'Yes.'

'Good. I'll give you his too, so that one day you might actually have a proper grown-up conversation about all this and sort yourselves out.'

'That's if he can squeeze me in.'

Noah was pouring boiling water on tea leaves but the sour tone got through. 'Ashley, you're sounding very bitter and it doesn't suit you. All the things you've gone through, and I've never heard you sound so self-pitying. Maybe it's about time you grew up.'

She was just about to launch into him when his phone rang. Fuming, she took Bronte outside. She was leaning against the wall of her sun terrace when Noah joined her. He passed her a mug of tea, his expression so shocked, she forgot to be angry with him.

'What is it? What's wrong? Is the family all right?'

'All fine at home. It's Petra,' he said. 'She's gone. Jumped ship. Left town.'

'What do you mean?' Ashley sank onto the low wall in shock, and sensitive Bronte picked up her mood and crept behind her knees, giving comfort.

'Remember the band at the station? And the way The Jenny WRENs sang so effortlessly with it?'

Ashley nodded.

'Turns out they've been rehearsing together for a while. When the coverage went out on *Focus Southwest* it created a load of publicity. The band had been about to go on tour, so they've decided to take The Jenny WRENs with them.'

'You mean she's just left everything here? Dropped the café in the lurch? Dropped you in the lurch? How could she!' Ashley was angry again but this time it was on behalf of her cousin. He looked utterly defeated. Despite his protestations that he and Petra were strictly casual, she suspected his feelings ran deeper. 'I knew she was up to something. She's been positively shifty lately. And bad-tempered.'

He joined her on the wall and sipped his tea disconsolately. 'Guilt, maybe? But come on, Ash, it's her big break. It's what she's always wanted to do.'

'You always see the best in everyone, and I've always admired that in you, but, you come on, she's treated us all like shit.' He didn't answer, just let his head hang. She gave him a hug. 'I'm sorry, Noah. I know you liked her.'

'I don't know if you know anything about her background?'

Ashley shook her head. 'Never discussed it.'

'Petra was brought up in care, as her mum couldn't cope, and there was no dad on the scene. She went through a series of foster homes, was pushed out into the world aged eighteen and had to find her own way. Worked her way through catering college, when all the time all she wanted to do was sing.'

'Poor Petra. I had no idea.' Ashley thought back to the argument at choir. As she recollected, she'd been moaning about how complicated life was. She thought of the comfortable house on the outskirts of Ludlow, the idyllic childhood her devoted parents had provided, the security of having a loving extended family around her, including a protective cousin. Petra had had none of that. For the first time it struck Ashley how alone the girl was. She'd never mentioned family or friends. And Ashley had never asked. How self-involved she'd been, bleating on. She could hear her self-pitying whine now and shuddered. Was it really such a big deal that Eddie was having a baby with Bree? Maybe it was time to pull on her big girl pants and face the situation head on. No wonder Petra had had little sympathy, no wonder she'd snapped.

'Poor Petra indeed. It means she doesn't see anything as permanent, doesn't like anything or anyone clinging to her. The proverbial rolling stone. The one thing she's worked solidly for is a singing career.' He shrugged. 'So she saw her chance and took it.'

'And she didn't want you clinging to her either? I'm sorry, coz.'

He scuffed his feet. 'Well, you know what they say, water under the bridge and all that.'

'Must hurt, though.'

'What must?'

She put an arm through his and looked up at him. She knew he'd bounce back. He always did. 'A woman so oblivious to your charms that, instead of staying in Berecombe and being wooed by you, she's chosen to tramp around the UK on tour with a big band.' She saw his mouth twitch.

They began to walk back into the flat. 'Has anyone told you that you have a very cruel streak, Ashley Ann Lydden? For that, you can wash up your own mugs.'

'Sorry. Did you like her a lot, then? I did; she was great fun. I still can't believe she kept it all a secret.'

'Ash, the woman hasn't died, she's just gone on tour. She'll be back.'

'Yes, but will Berecombe welcome her back? I can only imagine what Biddy will say about all this. Oh!' Ashley stopped in the doorway to the sitting room, putting her hand to her mouth in horror. 'Noah, it's the tea dance on Thursday at the café. What the hell are we going to do without Petra? I'd better make some emergency phone calls!'

Chapter Twenty-Six

When Ashley got to the café on the morning of the tea dance, the Berecombe community had sprung into action. A gang comprising Biddy, Beryl, Tessa, Eleri, Zoe and Millie – holding her newborn – were all there. Also present were Elvis, and Trevor, Millie's little cockapoo, who both nosed Bronte with interest.

Biddy, of course, assumed command. 'Ah, Ashley. You're here. Right, listen up, ladies, here's the plan of action for today. Beryl, myself and Tessa will man the kitchen. Zoe, you're in charge of music. Eleri, can you waitress?'

'No problem, Biddy.' The spectacular-looking woman with the waist-length wavy hair and sea-green eyes winked at Millie. 'It'll be just like old times, won't it, *cariad*?'

'What can I do, Biddy?' Millie asked.

'You, young lady, can sit in the shade and look after your little Edie,' Biddy ordered sternly. 'You're not to lift a finger.'

'I've got to help. It's my café!'

'And exactly how old is that baby?'

'Eight weeks today.'

'Precisely. You have given birth eight weeks ago. I will not have you rushing about the place, tiring yourself out when you've got a baby to look after.'

'Aw, come on, Biddy. She sleeps most of the time.'

'I insist,' the older woman answered, in a tone which brooked no opposition.

Ashley, seeing Millie's frustration, jumped in. 'The menu's agreed – we kept it simple, thank goodness – and there's a list in the kitchen. Supplies should all be in there too. What can I do? I can't waitress, unfortunately – my balance still isn't good – but I could help in the kitchen. Washing up, maybe?'

'Only those with Food Hygiene Level Two allowed in the kitchen,' Biddy barked. 'And I don't suppose that's you, is it?'

'No,' Ashley said faintly, in awe of Biddy in full Boadicea mode.

'Then you can set up the tables and chairs. Don't forget the parasols – it's going to be a hot one today –

and make sure Millie doesn't move.' Biddy pointed an authoritarian finger. 'You can both be in charge of taking the tickets, and make sure no one comes in who hasn't been invited. Arthur will be along later to act as security.'

There were one or two raised eyebrows at the thought of the mild-mannered Arthur being 'on the door'.

Biddy swept them with an imperious look. 'No doubt there'll be some folk who will try to get in for a free cake and cuppa. How many are we expecting?'

'I allocated all the available tickets, so there should be sixty guests coming, plus we'll have to cater for the Jitter Boogies who are coming to do a demo dance.' As Biddy raised an eyebrow in enquiry, Ashley added meekly, 'There are eight of them.'

Biddy nodded. 'So, if we aim to cater for eighty that will include us. Army can't march on an empty stomach, can it? Right, everyone know what they're doing?'

'Yes, Biddy.'

'I didn't hear that. Speak up, say it with conviction. Everyone know what they're doing?'

'YES, BIDDY!'

'Right then, stir your stumps. Let's save this tea dance from disaster!'

Ashley looked around a little helplessly. 'She's a magnificent woman,' she said to Millie. 'I thought this was my project.'

Millie giggled. 'She's that, all right. Now, how do you want this space sorted? Oh hang on, can you help, Zoe? I think Miss Edie is requesting a feed.' She sat and fed the baby as Ashley and Zoe arranged tables and chairs around the edge, leaving a large space in the middle for dancing. In the shade by the bookshop they were setting up a couple of tables and umbrellas as a ticket collecting station when Jed, Millie's husband, arrived, struggling with a large wooden structure.

'Where can I put this?'

'What is it?' Zoe asked.

'It's a wooden playpen. A present from my esteemed mother.'

Millie came up to them, holding a milk-drunk baby. She kissed her husband. 'Only, as I decided no child of mine is going to be held captive, I thought it would be ideal as a dog creche. We've already got three dogs here and when Arthur arrives, that'll be Daisy too. Not that any of them are any trouble, but it'll save us having to keep an eye on where they are and, in Trevor's case, what he's scrounging off the guests.'

Zoe laughed. 'Brilliant idea. Hand it over, Jed. Where do you want it, Ash?'

'Set it up next to the wall there. Out of the way.'

'And shadier than a very shady place. I'll get them a nice big bowl of water too.'

Jed kissed his wife and touched a loving finger to his daughter's downy head. 'Don't work,' he warned. 'I wish I could stay and help, but you know I have to get to this meeting.'

'We'll be fine. Ashley, here, has been assigned as my bodyguard, so I won't move a muscle. All we'll be doing is checking tickets and handing guests over to Eleri.' They kissed again and he left, reluctance evident in every muscle.

With Trevor, Elvis and Bronte established in the dog creche, Millie and Ashley sat at their table and sipped the chilled homemade lemonade Zoe had brought over.

'Are you okay, Zoe?' Ashley asked. 'I know Jake is in London.'

'Yeah. Some big commission. Good for his career.'

Millie glanced, with narrowed eyes, from one to the other. 'Am I missing something here?'

'Ashley thinks I'm all miz because I went out with Jake once or twice and now he's gone. Don't worry, Ash, I'm not broken-hearted. It would take a weaker woman than me to fall for his cheese.' She pulled a face. 'Even if he was an ace kisser.' Turning on her heel, she flapped a seagull away and then concentrated on putting out baskets of pink serviettes.

'That told me,' Ashley murmured.

Millie laughed. 'One day Zoe will fall properly in

love, but it hasn't happened yet. I can't decide if the man will be lucky or cursed.' She switched her gaze to the baby in her arms. 'You know, little one, your daddy and I decided on Edie as one of your names, but I'm still not sure it suits you.'

Ashley glanced over warily. Fear prickled. She wasn't comfortable around babies; it brought her childless state into too sharp a focus. 'She might grow into it.'

'Her middle name's Roberta. *The Railway Children* was one of my favourite books when I was a kid.'

'Not sure that's right either,' Ashley replied, treading carefully. 'Perhaps she can decide what she wants to be called when she's older? I went through a phase, when I was ten, of only answering to Buffy. Obsessed with the TV series,' she added as explanation.

'Ooh, so was I,' Millie replied. 'Although I was a Willow fan. I loved how she was always in the library looking stuff up.'

'And Giles!' the two women said simultaneously.

'My first crush,' Ashley said dreamily. Perhaps she was destined to fall for academics? She'd loved Giles when she was a pre-teen, now she loved Eddie. The thought shocked her into silence. Did she love Eddie? Maybe. And now it looked like, due to her stupidity, she'd never find out if there could be a future for them. She eyed the infant in Millie's arms, pretending she was

Eddie's. She could cope with the situation, couldn't she? If it meant being with Eddie? Or at least give it a go. Her phone was wedged into the back pocket of her jeans; she could feel it pressing against her back. She could ring him right now.

'I don't think she looks like a Giles either,' Millie said, laughing, breaking into Ashley's thoughts.

'She definitely doesn't look like a Giles. She's beautiful.' Ashley sat up. 'Wasn't Roberta called Bobbie in *The Railway Children*? I mean, I haven't read the book, only seen the film. What about Bobbie?'

Millie rocked her baby gently. 'Bobbie. Bobbie the baby! Ashley, you're a genius. She looks just like a Bobbie. What do think, Bobbie? Do you think it suits you? We'll have to run it past your daddy, and I know it'll annoy the hell out of Granny Henville, which can only be a good thing. Oof, take her for a second, will you? She's getting heavy. I could murder a cup of tea. I'll get you one too.' She placed the baby into the crook of Ashley's arm.

'I don't... I can't... I haven't a clue about babies,' Ashley spluttered, horrified at how wonderful the baby's weight felt in her arms.

'Neither had I until eight weeks ago,' Millie said cheerfully. 'I think instinct kicks in. I was never around babies much, so I didn't know what to do either. Just support her head and come and get me if she starts to grizzle.'

She was heading into the café before Ashley had time to protest further.

She sat in the quiet of the morning, listening to the snuffly breathing of the baby in her arms, not daring to move in case she woke her up. Ashley stared in fascination. Her eyelids were almost translucent, her lashes a dark crescent on her flushed, rounded cheeks. The rosebud mouth worked, as if dreaming of milk and kisses. Inching her hand closer, Ashley touched one tiny finger, complete with a pearly-shell fingernail, and was rewarded with a grip as the baby held on. She was a perfect human in miniature. A miracle. Ashley felt the knot of need harden in her empty womb. She wanted one. She wanted one of these and, worse, she wanted the father to be Eddie. A tear rolled silently down her face. Eddie deserved to know the truth about her, that it would be unlikely she could give him any more children. Would he feel the same way about her then? And could she really help to bring up his son, knowing she couldn't have a baby of her own?

'There, what did I say?' Millie said, as she returned with two mugs of tea. 'You've got the hang of it. Look like a natural. What's the matter? Oh Ashley, I didn't mean to upset you. What have I said?'

Ashley handed over the baby and grabbed a serviette to wipe her tears away. 'You haven't said anything. Oh Millie,' she blurted, 'I've been told I probably can't have babies, and I'm finding it hard to deal with.' The tears fell and her shoulders shook with sobs. 'I so loved holding Edie, I mean Bobbie, but it's the worst feeling too, as I'll probably never have one of my own.'

Millie settled the baby in her buggy, found a packet of tissues, handed them over and waited. When Ashley had recovered, she said, 'I'm so sorry. So thoughtless of me. I would never have asked you to hold her, had I known.' She pushed the mug of tea nearer. 'Here, drink this, my lovely. Always helps.'

'Thanks, Millie,' Ashley hiccoughed. 'I'm sorry to fall apart on you. Bobbie is a gorgeous baby. It's just—'

'She's not yours. I understand. Do you want to tell me about it? You can tell me to mind my own beeswax if you want, but I'm a good listener.'

As Ashley haltingly told her about the extent of her injuries and about the consultant's warning, she thought how good it felt to talk to Millie. She wasn't a live-in-the-moment-take-everything-casual girl like Petra, or sympathetic-but-male like Noah. She simply listened, didn't interrupt and Ashley had the feeling she really did understand.

'Mmm,' Millie said, when she'd finished. 'Sounds to

me as if the consultant is hedging his bets. Doesn't sound as if anything's certain until you're further along being healed. And, if you don't mind my saying, it sounds as if you might be projecting your fear of getting pregnant onto the situation too. Hardly surprising, considering the trauma you've been through. Pelvic injuries need to be taken seriously when considering pregnancy, I would imagine.' She winced. 'It's a hell of a strain on that part of your anatomy, I can tell you. Your body's let you down, too, and that's doubly hard, seeing as beforehand you'd got it all – a career, a boyfriend, a healthy body.'

'That I totally took for granted.'

'But we do, don't we? You're about my age, aren't you? I took for granted what my body could and couldn't do, and then I went through pregnancy and giving birth and now,' she cast a doting look at her daughter, 'now I know my body's amazing. It can produce this little darling.' She twisted and took Ashley's hands in hers. 'I also think you should give yourself time. Your body may be healing but your mind probably hasn't caught up. Take it a little easier on yourself, my lovely. Don't make any big decisions.' At Ashley's strangled laugh, she added, 'What? What have I said now? Oh, is this about Eddie and Bree? This town is a shocking rumour mill, worse than any village.'

'I'm not sure I can make the compromise.' Ashley

glanced at the baby, serenely asleep in her pushchair, and could feel the soft weight in her arms again. 'I thought I could, but holding Bobbie brought things into sharp relief. Things have got complicated and Eddie and I still haven't talked.'

'And talking is the thing you need to do. Tricky, though, when he keeps haring off to the USA. I heard he's back there now.'

'Is he?' Ashley asked, shocked. Eddie hadn't been in touch but she'd assumed he was busy with the TV programme. 'I didn't know. It must be something to do with the baby.'

'When's it due?'

'September sometime, I think. I'm not really sure.' God, she'd been self-involved. She didn't even know when Eddie's son was due to be born.

'Maybe there's a problem with the pregnancy and he's gone early to support Bree?' Millie sat back on her chair and adjusted her sunglasses. 'Babies don't tend to fit neatly into a life-plan, no matter how much you want them to; they arrive when they're ready. I suppose you had a life-plan?'

Ashley nodded. 'Oh yes. Get to departmental head, marry Piers – that was the bloke who ran out on me as soon as I couldn't. Run, that is. Get five years under my belt as head of art, have three babies by the time I was forty and go part-time to enjoy them.'

'Don't they say life happens when you're too busy making plans?' Millie offered. She pointed to the flat above the café. 'I lived there with my parents. All set to go off to university, but then they died, so I took over the café. I've had my worst times in this place but the best of all times too. And then Jed came along and I couldn't trust him enough to let him in. Thought he was the enemy, you see, right up until the very last moment, when I realised he was my hero – and even then I fought him. Pride wouldn't let me date a rich guy.'

They laughed.

'I suppose what I'm saying is, sometimes you have to let Fate take you the way it wants. And sometimes it takes you in very surprising directions. If you'd told me two years ago that I'd be married with a baby and living in the most idyllic country cottage with a man who worships me, I would've told you to take a running jump off the harbour wall. If you're still adapting to your life-plan not working out, then just sit back and let go. You're probably still mourning its loss. If in doubt, do nothing. But,' she added hastily, 'I'd definitely try to sit Eddie down and talk to him at some point.'

'So everyone keeps telling me. You've said a lot of things that make sense, Millie. Stuff about me being hard on myself, that I've lost trust in my body. You're a wise woman.'

'The vampire slayer taught me well,' Millie said solemnly. 'Come here, have a hug.'

They hugged and Ashley clung on, tears threatening again.

'All good?' Millie asked.

Ashley nodded.

'Then, as I can see Ruby and Arthur heading our way, let's get on with our totally onerous and underpaid task of checking them in.'

Chapter Twenty-Seven

In the end it all went well. Ashley should have known the Berecombe community would rise to the occasion, but there'd been no guarantee anyone would turn up after her panicked phone calls the other night. It had been the perfect weather for it; the late July sun shone hot, but there was a cooling breeze coming off the sea. Their guests enjoyed cucumber sandwiches and copious amounts of tea and ginger beer, scones with rich Devon clotted cream and tiny fairy cakes decorated with red, white and blue icing. The Jitter Boogies performed an awe-inspiring jitterbug routine that had them all gasping in admiration, and afterwards Zoe played gentler music designed for something slower-paced.

Ashley, watching from her shady position, felt the weight of responsibility slip off her shoulders. The organisation today had been all down to Biddy, and the woman had seized control with relish, but the lead-up had been down to Ashley and Petra. Even though Ashley was still cross with her friend for running out, she wished she'd been there to enjoy it; it had been a fabulous day. Most guests had now left and Arthur and Beryl were dancing a lazy waltz. Ashley let herself drift with the late afternoon heat but was roused by Ruby's voice.

'Ashley dearie, have you got that recorder thingy with you? Victor's got to talking and I think it'll be a smashing memory to add.'

Rummaging around in her rucksack, Ashley fished out the handheld and set it up on a table in between two chairs in a quiet corner of the patio. She made more tea and took it to them, along with a plate of biscuits. Taking her own mug, she went to sit on the low wall overlooking the beach. Over the happy sounds of families enjoying the beach, she could hear Biddy loudly organising the clearing up. *That woman really should run for prime minister,* she thought with a smile.

She drank in a cleansing breath of invigorating sea air. Maybe it was time to ring Eddie. As her finger hovered over his number, ready to press 'call', her phone buzzed and his name flashed across the screen. Heart thumping, she answered. 'Hello, Eddie.'

'Hi.' He sounded exhausted.

'Are you all right?'

'Bree's had the baby.'

Ashley swallowed. She could do this. Be a grown-up. 'That's great news,' she said cautiously. 'Congratulations. Mum and baby okay? Sounds like the baby was early.'

'Both are fine and healthy but, yeah, the baby was early. Took us all by surprise.'

'How are you?'

'I don't know. Spaced out, walking on air, so tired I could sleep for a week. Exhilarated. Proud.'

Ashley smiled. He sounded all of those things and more.

'I wish you were here. Jeez, that sounds self-centred, but I could do with you here right now.'

A lump lodged in her throat. 'I've missed you too.'

'Have you?'

'Yes. Oh Eddie, there are so many things I want to tell you. But not over the phone. Not now. This is yours and the baby's time. You…' Her voice began to break; this was harder than she'd thought. 'You need to look after Bree.' She steered things back to the less emotional. 'Has the baby got a name yet?'

'Bree decided on Hal.'

'Hal McQueen?'

'No, it'll be Bauer. Bree's decided the baby will take her surname.'

She felt for him, recollecting Petra's theory that Bree was simply using him. Had she been right? 'Hal Bauer. Sounds good. What's he like?'

'Perfect. Oh Ash, he's perfect.'

'Does he look like you?'

'No, he's all his mom. Long legs with dark hair, like Bree. I'll send a photo.'

Her thoughts flitted back to holding Millie's tiny daughter. The soft weight and the unique baby smell. There might be a time when she held little Hal. He was part of Eddie and she loved the man. She could love his son too, couldn't she? 'Where are you? I can hear birds and traffic.'

'Sitting on a bench in Brigham's gardens.'

'Brigham?'

'Hospital in Boston. Grabbing a break. Mom and Dad are visiting soon, so I don't have long. Guess I'll stay with Bree and Hal for a month or so, but I've got to get back for filming in the fall. It'll be tough.'

'It will. You won't want to leave the baby. But, on a very selfish note, I can't wait to see you.'

'After the train ride I wasn't sure how you felt. You still seemed pissed at me.'

'That was a misunderstanding. I didn't make myself

clear about Jake... about a lot of things.' She sucked in a breath. 'Eddie, there are reasons I've been behaving so irrationally. But,' she sighed, exasperated, 'it's so difficult to find the words, especially on the phone.'

'I'll be back in September. We'll talk then, I promise, and I'll listen to everything you have to say. I want to hear it, Ash. I want to work things out between us. Any way we can.'

The fear slipped from her shoulders. Maybe they could do this? Relief warmed her voice. 'So do I. Oh Eddie, so do I.'

'You have no idea how good that is to hear.' He sounded emotional. 'I—' he began but paused.

Ashley could almost hear him thinking. There was silence for a few seconds and she thought the connection had died.

Then he cleared his throat. 'Now, tell me, what's happening in Berecombe? How did the tea dance go?'

She was touched that he remembered, but then, of course he would. The hot, fierce longing for him returned but it was layered now with a tenderness she'd never felt for any other man. 'You really want to hear about little old Berecombe now?'

'Trust me, it'll make a change from timing contractions and staring at monitors and graphs.'

She laughed a little. 'Well, Petra got the offer of a singing tour with a band, so ran out on us.'

'Aw, jeez!'

'But the Berecombe community rallied round and the tea dance was a success. Two GIs came and good old Victor is still here.'

'Describe what's happening.'

'You really want to hear about Devon when you've just become a father?'

'I just want to hear your voice, Ashley.'

She looked around. 'Okay then.' Using her painter's eye, she began. 'I'm at the café. It's just gone six. The tide is on the way out, and when the beach is quieter we're going to take the dogs for a run. Oh yes, I got a dog! I'm not sure if you'll have heard that yet. There are still a lot of people on the sand, as it's been such a lovely day.' She put a hand to her eyes, shielding them from the low sun. 'There's a dinghy race or something going on and there's quite a crowd watching from the harbour. It's not as hazy, now the worst of the heat has gone. I think we'll have a good sunset.'

'It was clear the day we met. On the bench when you jumped at the noise of the crashing cars and all your painting stuff fell on the ground.'

Ashley smiled. 'It was. Seems such a long time ago now.'

'Only February.'

'So much has happened.'

'It has, and yet nothing has.'

Ashley could hear the longing in his voice.

'Tell me some more.'

Ashley twisted to look at the café. 'I'm sitting on the wall of the patio. Victor and Ruby are chatting over a mug of tea.'

'Tea. Of course.'

'Well, you know us Brits run on tea. All the other guests have gone home. I can hear Biddy in the kitchen. Beryl is watching Arthur teach Zoe a few jitterbug steps – he's surprisingly nimble on his feet. Millie is sitting in the shade with her new baby on her shoulder.' Ashley tried to keep the yearning out of her voice. 'She's wrapped in a white shawl and has her head on mum's shoulder. Eleri is sitting with them.'

'Eleri?'

'Millie's friend and sort-of sister-in-law. She runs The Henville. Goes out with Alex Henville.'

'Oh yes, of course.'

'Tessa and Ken are feeding the dogs in the doggie creche.'

'Doggie creche?'

'Don't ask. The scent of fish and chips is floating over

from The Plaice Place and making me long for something savoury after all the fairy cakes.'

'Cupcakes.'

'Fairy cakes,' she corrected.

'Okay, you got it, fairy cakes,' he conceded on a laugh.

'The sun's in the west and making everything glow golden. It's picking up the red cliffs at West Bay, and I can just see Portland shimmering in the distance. Oh, and Jed and Noah have just arrived. They're taking orders for fish and chips. Zoe's put some more music on and it looks like Noah has a bottle of champagne. Amy's locked up the bookshop and is heading over. It looks like we're having a party. Would you like me to tell them the baby news? I'm sure they'd like to congratulate you.'

'Sure. Go ahead.'

She held her phone out. 'Everyone, listen. Bree has had the baby. A baby boy. Eddie is now a father.' The cheering echoed and bounced around the walls.

'Tell him huge congratulations,' yelled Noah, as he wrestled with the champagne cork. 'And that we're wetting the baby's head.' The cork shot out with a huge pop and everyone cheered again. 'You okay?' he mouthed to Ashley and she nodded.

Putting the phone back to her ear, she said, 'Did you get all that?'

'I did. I'm picturing it and wishing I was with you all. With you.'

'I do too,' she whispered. 'Look, about Jake—'

'We'll talk in September,' he said firmly. 'I ought to get back to Bree, and my mom and dad will be here any minute. Oh God, Ash, I just have so much I want to say to you.'

'I'll be waiting, Eddie. I'll be here in Berecombe waiting for you. It'll be our time then.'

'Oh Ashley, come September it'll definitely be our time.' The phone went silent.

September. The word held such promise.

For a teacher, the month was always about new beginnings. And it would be a new beginning for her and Eddie. She was sure of it. With a smile on her face and hope bursting in her heart, she turned away from where the sea danced diamonds and joined the party.

Acknowledgments

I needed a lot of help to write this one! I hope I've included everyone this time.

My sincere thanks go to the very lovely and talented Colin Simmonds who furnished me with details of a painter's life, and to Dr Pinky Jain and Dr Linzi McKerr of Worcester University for information on academia. My grateful thanks go to Julia Roebuck who opened up the world of Morris Dancing, Wendy Jones who, as always, gave medical information, and Leah Larson and Greg Poulos for help on all things USA. Janice Rosser and the Helen Vereker Singers helped with what it means to be in a community choir and Janice Preston provided information about art classes. Thank you all! I'm also grateful that writing this book meant I had an excuse to discuss my mother's childhood wartime memories with her. She also helped with the titles. Thanks mum! I'm so grateful these people gave up their precious time to share their expertise; any mistakes are very much all mine.

Charlotte Ledger and her team at One More Chapter helped shape this book with brilliant editing and I am eternally grateful for their enthusiasm and expertise.

And finally, a huge thank you to you, the reader, for buying, borrowing, reading, reviewing, and supporting my books. If one thing the past two years have proved, it's that reading and books are more important than ever.

Return to Berecombe and find out what happens next in *Blue Skies and Blackberry Pies*!

Berecombe's year of commemoration may be coming to a close … but the rest of Ashley Lydden's new life has only just begun! Ashley couldn't have predicted that she'd find herself a whole new – much happier – life in the quiet seaside town of Berecombe, but now she can't imagine being anywhere else.

She knows better than most though that life has a way of surprising you when you least expect it…

Read on for an exclusive excerpt of Part 3: *Blue Skies and Blackberry Pies*...

The Berecombe News
OUR FABULOUS YEAR OF COMMEMORATION CONTINUES!
By: Keeley Sharma

As well as mists and mellow fruitfulness, this autumn also brings our very own film festival, co-ordinated by Patron of the Regent Theatre, Michael Love. Mike is born-and-bred Berecombe and is now a theatre director of international repute. He promises there will be a film to tempt everyone's tastes. Speaking of tastes, Nico, from the Icicle Works, is concocting a special flavour of ice-cream for the intervals. Let's hope it's not World War Two themed or we might end up with frozen carrot and potato in our cone!

The year culminates in the opening of Berecombe Museum's Living Memories Exhibition. Museum director Noah Lydden assures me it will be fascinating to anyone with an interest in the history of our wonderful town. There's a party on the first night, attendance strictly by invitation, which is bound to be a great night, as we all know how much Berecombe likes to party. And speaking of which, I hear a street party has been organised, too. Get that bunting out!

There has been a real sense of community working together

this year and we should all be proud of how our little town has commemorated the seventy-fifth anniversary of the D-Day landings.

Look out for a special picture edition of **The Berecombe News** *to celebrate this most special of years.*

Chapter One

Ashley cycled along Berecombe seafront, breathing in great gulps of salty Devon air. It was a detour from her flat to the Arts Workshop but, on a day like today, it was too good to miss. Making sure she didn't cycle too fast, as Bronte's lead was attached to the handlebars and she was running alongside, she stole a glance at the view. Now that the school holidays were over, most of the visitors she could see were retired, or young couples with pre-school-age children enjoying the beach and making the most of the blue skies and warm sunshine. The summer had been a series of long, hot, sunny days running into one another. And now, although it was early September, the weather was still balmy. It was possibly even better now that the shrill heat of July and August was softened by gentle breezes. As she slowly cycled she could hear the shrieks and giggles of children building sandcastles or paddling in Berecombe's safe, shallow waters.

Stopping to better enjoy the view, she checked on the little black poodle panting beside her. She was on her way to teach her first art class. Nerves suddenly hit; she hadn't taught for over two years. 'Ooh, Bronte, let's just hope I haven't forgotten how to do it!' she murmured.

Lifting her face to the sun for a few luxurious seconds, she inhaled the soothing sea air and concentrated on slowing her breathing and calming herself down. The sea sparkled a dancing blue, pillowy clouds drifted and all around her were the happy sounds and intoxicating smells of a seaside town. Not for the first time she thanked her lucky stars that she'd ended up living in this quirky little town in east Devon. It had helped her heal, she'd made new friends and had a job she loved. And now she was about to take another step on the road to getting back to herself. No, she corrected. She was taking another leap into creating the new her! Her nerves were replaced by an enormous sense of well-being as with a grin she pushed off and headed for the Workshop.

An hour later, she faced the class in airy Studio One. It was a group of only nine and all women. Easels and chairs had been set up in a circle around a tableau of three white jugs sitting on some rich blue velvet with a bowl of vivid oranges. The colours popped and zinged and, along with the familiar scent of paint tickling her nostrils, took her straight back into her teaching days before her accident. She just hoped she could still do it. Forcing herself to relax, she remembered what Ken, her manager, had whispered to her on the way in. 'Remember, it's not like teaching schoolkids – they all want to be here. Or that's the theory.'

Ashley hoped so. At least her friend Beryl was here. The woman, dressed today in a bright pink linen smock and matching earrings, which contrasted with her silver pixie cut, gave her an encouraging wave as she sat down at one of the easels. Ashley smiled back. Beryl and Biddy, Berecombe's most notorious pensioners, had become two of her closest friends. She was particularly fond of Beryl. Biddy could be forthright and difficult, but Beryl was nothing but kindness and Ashley knew she was here to show moral support. If someone had told her two years ago that she'd be best buds with a couple of women well into their seventies, she would have laughed. But they'd become family – her family in Berecombe. She watched as the rest of the group settled. The only other woman she knew was Marti Cavendish from choir, who was chatting to a sleek middle-aged woman in expensive-looking white jeans. Ashley winced. Perhaps the first lesson might be about what was appropriate to wear in an art studio.

Ashley hesitated, wondering when the best time would be to bring the class to order. She couldn't believe how nervous she felt – her legs were trembling! She'd been teaching art all her working life, and even though

Ken had said they differed from schoolchildren in that they'd paid to be here, that might well mean they'd be more demanding. Beryl caught her eye and winked. It gave her a little courage. No going back now.

Clearing her throat, she began to speak. 'If you could all face the front, then we can start.' No response, they were all too busy chatting. Oh God, it was going to be a disaster, wasn't it? What could she do? Taking a deep breath, Ashley dipped into her teacher's bag of tricks and summoned up her alter ego, the one she used to use to best effect with the tricky Year Nines on a wet Thursday afternoon. 'Right then,' she bellowed, making them all jump. 'Face this way, ladies, and we'll get going.' It worked. Even Marti stopped gossiping and faced the front. Teaching, Ashley suddenly remembered, was all about acting a part. Forcing yourself into the authority role and beaming out confident vibes even when, as now, it was the last thing you felt. She felt her shoulders loosen as she realised they were sitting up and paying attention. Out of the corner of her eye, she saw Beryl give her the thumbs-up. A rush of confidence flooded through her as she settled back into the old, familiar groove. She might not have taught for some time, but it was like riding a bike; she hadn't lost it after all.

Lowering the volume to a more conversational and friendly level, she said, 'We'll begin by introducing ourselves. I'll start. My name is Ashley Lydden. I've taught art for all of my teaching career, although I'll confess, this is my first class for a while.' Again, at the perimeter of her vision, she saw Beryl nod encouragingly. Forcing a smile, she added, 'I hope you'll forgive me if I'm a little rusty.' She was relieved to see that there were one or two sympathetic murmurs. They were on her side. Emboldened, she went on. 'You see, I had a car accident a while ago which meant I had to learn how to walk again.' A shocked sound rippled around the room. 'It also meant I couldn't stand for any length of time so I couldn't teach.' Ashley let out a breath. There was a time when she couldn't tell even her closest friends about the accident and now she was telling a room full of strangers. Realising how far she'd come in her recovery thrilled her. That and being back in an art studio and teaching. It was a wonderful feeling. She relaxed some more. She could do this! 'So, if I pull up a stool next to where you're working and sit on it peering over your shoulder, please don't be put off. It's just a more comfortable way for me to give you some feedback and tips.' Relieved laughter sounded and she felt her nerves calm. She'd definitely got them on side. Now she could take them with her on their learning journey. Oh, how she'd missed this. She hadn't actually known how much until this moment.

'After you've introduced yourselves, I'm going to set you a task so I can see how you work. It'll give me a good idea how to tailor the next lessons so I can best move you on. Remember, none of this is about competition.' At this Marti looked disappointed. 'It's about exploring and developing your own personal style and using a range of media and techniques. But most of all, it's about having fun!'

At the half-time break, Ken popped into Studio One to see how everything was going. 'Okay?' he asked.

'Think so,' she whispered. 'I remembered to do the health and safety and fire drill stuff, had a chat about wearing old clothes or bringing an old shirt, doled out the obligatory painting kit to those who thought it would be provided, and set them to a still life. Not very exciting but it gives me a chance to evaluate their skills. See what I'm working with.'

'Excellent idea. I watched a little of the session through the window just in case you needed me to jump in but there was no need. You handle them really well, Ashley, my friend. Just the right amount of encouragement and suggestion on how to improve. I didn't expect anything less.' As he saw Beryl approach, he added, 'I'll leave you to it. Looks like you've got it all under control. And, if it helps, imagine them all—'

'Naked. Yes, thanks, Ken. And it doesn't!'

He grinned, put up his hands in surrender and left.

'I've brought you a coffee,' Beryl said, handing over a mug. 'You're doing so well, my lovely. I've heard lots of compliments about how good a teacher you are.'

'Thanks, Beryl. I was so nervous at the start!'

'Absolutely no need and I can assure you it didn't show. We're all having a super time and learning lots.'

'I can't tell you how relieved I am that it's going well, and I *really* appreciate you coming along.' She glanced over to where the students had gathered around the hot water urn. 'I'm not sure if I ought to go and mingle at the tea table or leave them to bond as a group. If they were schoolkids, I'd leave them to it but—'

'Oh, they'll come over when they're ready. And in Marti's case, it'll be to tell you how she narrowly missed out on getting into the Royal College of Art. She's already bored that nice lady wearing the white jeans.' Beryl winked, her wrinkles creasing into well-worn grooves. 'I'm amazed she's had time to fit everything she claims to have done into such a short life, especially as she only admits to thirty-nine.'

They laughed. Marti was well known for her boastful ways.

'I'm really enjoying this,' Beryl continued. 'Thanks for putting the class on. I'm missing choir ever since Petra left, so it fills a gap. And it's good to flex the old creative skills. If I have any.'

'I had a sneaky look when you popped to the loo. You've got talent, Beryl. And thank you for the kind words. If this goes well, I'll think about putting on more classes, maybe some in the evening for those not free during the day.'

'Excellent idea.'

'I miss choir, too,' Ashley said, as she sipped her coffee. 'I loved those fun sing-alongs, especially the *Grease* medleys. Always left in such a good mood. Really lifted the spirits.'

'Have you heard from Petra?'

Petra, Ashley's friend who had been running the choir, had recently skipped town unexpectedly.

'No. I imagine she's too busy. Touring the country with the band – going from town to town – can't leave much time spare.' Ashley supposed it was true, but she'd been disappointed that Petra hadn't rung. She'd thought they'd become close since she'd moved to Berecombe, and had considered Petra a good friend, so her sudden departure and radio silence ever since were hard for Ashley to process.

'Biddy's spitting feathers, she's that mad about the

girl running off and leaving everyone in the lurch.'

'And no one wants to get on the wrong side of Biddy.'

'I have to agree. Although she's one of my dearest friends, I confess to treading warily around her.'

'At least the café is in safe hands with Tessa, Eleri and Zoe – though I know Petra's managerial skills are sorely missed. I think they're planning to carry on until Millie finds a new manager to take over Petra's job.'

'And at least Tess can use the kitchen to make her bread. I'm particularly fond of her walnut loaf. It's not ideal though. The girl really should have given poor Millie some notice. Sorry, Ashley, I know she's a friend of yours.'

'Was. I haven't heard from her since she left and she didn't tell me anything about going off to sing with the band.'

'How hurtful. And what about your nice young man? Is Eddie returning to Berecombe soon?'

'I hope so. He's hoping to spend some time in town when he gets back from the States and before he has to go to Bristol to start filming.'

'I'm so looking forward to this TV series he's doing. Folklore and myth! Right up my alley. Now, you must excuse me, I'm just going to say hello to one or two people.'

Ashley watched her go. Beryl's question about Eddie

had made her insides go to mush in excitement. She couldn't wait to see him. As soon as they'd met, the attraction had been instant – and hot – but the relationship had been fraught with difficulties. Now, though, there was gentle hope on the horizon. Although not finding it easy, Ashley was gradually making peace with the fact that his ex-girlfriend was having his baby, and she had fully supported Eddie flying over to the States to be with Bree while she gave birth. They'd been in constant touch while he'd been in the US, but the time difference and his new baby made it difficult to talk.

Bree hadn't coped well after the birth, so they'd all gone to stay with Eddie's parents in Rockport, and he was leaving her and baby Hal there when he returned to the UK to make his new TV series. The set-up at Eddie's parents' sounded very cosy and Ashley was working hard at squashing down the jealousy; she felt very much the outsider – the other woman, even.

'Baby steps,' she muttered to herself, ignoring the irony. 'Baby steps.' This was one more thing she had to work on: coping with the fact that her new boyfriend had recently had a baby with another woman. Straightening her shoulders, she decided at this moment that she needed to concentrate on her job and wade in and get to know her class better. Heading over to the tea table, she went in search of more coffee and small talk.

Chapter Two

'Ashley? It's Petra.'

Ashley swung her legs off the sofa in shock, dislodging a grumbling Bronte. She was in her tiny flat and half-asleep, having indulged in a snooze before making supper. Holding the phone closer to her ear, she said, 'Hello, stranger.'

'Suppose I deserve that.'

'Well, yeah. You could have told me that you were planning on disappearing, Petra.' She heard a huge sigh at the other end of the line.

'I know. I got myself in a right old state about it. On one hand all I could see was my big break. Singing with the band and The Jenny WRENs to audiences who actually wanted to hear us, had *paid* to listen. It's all I've ever wanted to do, Ash. But then, there was the café... and Millie... and Berecombe. God, I love that town.'

'People are really missing choir.'

'I miss choir, too.'

Ashley heard a wobble in the voice. 'Beryl was saying at art class today how much she misses it. I do, too. I miss *you*, Petra.'

Petra gulped. 'I miss you, too, girlfriend. I can't believe you're being so nice to me. I don't deserve it. I've been meaning to ring for ages but kept putting it off. I didn't know how you'd feel about what I did. I bet the rest of Berecombe are baying for my blood, though.'

'Noah filled me in on a little bit of your childhood. About you being brought up in care. He said it's left you feeling as if you don't want to commit to anything, not on a permanent basis. He also explained how singing has been your dream for a long time. I sort of understand. I think. You could have talked to me, you know.'

'I know. But the way I grew up means you only have yourself to rely on. I don't find it easy to talk about myself.'

'Not even to your friends?'

'Am I still your friend, Ash?'

'Of course you are! I meant what I said, I really miss you. Place isn't the same without you.' She heard Petra blow her nose and gain some control.

'How's the caff?' she managed eventually.

'Millie's interviewing for a new café manager. In the meantime, Tessa, Eleri and Zoe are running it between them. Think Millie is hoping to get someone in before Zoe goes back to university in October.'

'I really messed them about, didn't I?'

'Well, yeah, to be honest, you did. But you know what folk in this town are like, they'll forgive you. When you come back all will be forgotten.'

'Even by Biddy?'

'Ah. Can't vouch for Biddy, although she might surprise you. She was amazing when we did the tea dance.'

'The tea dance! How did it go?'

Ashley thought back to the afternoon she and Petra had planned together as a tribute to the GIs who were staying in town as part of the D-Day seventy-fifth anniversary, and smiled. They'd had great fun working together on what food to serve, what music to play and who to invite, but Petra had left town before the event. 'It was a triumph. Your menu worked a treat, everyone danced and the sun shone. You would have been proud of how everyone came together to make it a success. But tell me about your tour. How's it all going? Hard work?'

'I'm knackered. Thought running the café was hard work but this is crazy. We spend hours in a van, all huddled up, get to some crappy digs, rehearse in a freezing-cold venue, perform, go to bed and then do it all over again the next day. The glamour of showbiz!'

'And you love it.'

'And I love it. One hundred per cent.' There was a pause. 'What's that scrabbling, chewing sort of a noise I can hear? Have you got mice?'

'It's Bronte, my poodle. She's chewing on the new toy I bought her on the way back from art class.'

'You've got a poodle? How did that come about?'

Ashley explained about the owner going into care and not being able to take her dog with her. 'So I adopted Bronte. Wouldn't be without her. She slept in her bed during the art class and was as good as gold. I was so proud of her.'

'She sounds lovely. I love Biddy's dog Elvis, so I can imagine she's just as cute. And what's this about an art class? Are you taking a class? Shouldn't think you need to.'

'Not taking, I'm *teaching* it.'

'Oh, Ash, you star, you. You go, girl! That's a huge step forward. I'm so pleased for you. Oh, I wish I was there to give you a great big hug.'

'Big hugs coming down the line right back atcha. I absolutely love it. Can't say it's as glam as your life but oh, Petra, it's so good to be back doing it again. I'm only doing four hours a week for now, but I'll build up if I can.'

'That's so great. How did the first class go?'

'Well, okay, I think.' Ashley felt a surge of pride as she remembered the comments from the students as they left. 'No, I *know* it went well. I got some really good feedback afterwards. I was nervous beforehand – thought I was going to be sick at one point and nearly backed out – but as soon as I started, it all began to come back. There's so much joy in pointing people towards how they could improve a skill. Only these are adults and not squelchy adolescents. Some of them are quite demanding and one really knows her art history. I definitely had to up my game but, you know what, I thoroughly enjoyed the challenge.'

'Sounds like you're getting your life back on track. I'm so pleased for you, hon.'

'Thanks. I think I am. I feel like things are slotting into place. Physically, I feel so much better, and after this first class, the confidence is coming back too. I really enjoyed it, but I have to confess it's exhausted me. Must be all the nervous energy I used up! I was having a snooze on the sofa when you rang. Not used to being on my feet so much. Plus, I've got Marti Cavendish in the class so she's keeping me on my toes, so to speak.'

'Not Marti! The opera star?'

'And now apparently Royal College of Art entrant. Her talents have no—'

'Beginning!' they said simultaneously and laughed.

'It's so good to talk to you, Petra.' Ashley felt a swell of emotion for her friend. She'd only got to know Petra since moving to Berecombe but they'd quickly become good friends and she'd been lonely since she left. 'You will keep in touch from now on, won't you? Oh, and ring my big coz Noah, will you? He'd love to hear from you. I know you and he had something going on between you before you went away, and I think he'd like to make it something more. Ooh, hang on, Bronte's barking. I've got to go, there's someone at the door. Ring me again when you can. I still haven't told you about me and Eddie.'

'Don't tell me things have finally moved on between you two?'

'Okay, I'm coming,' Ashley called towards the door. 'Bronte, stop barking. Look, I've got to go, the dog's going nuts. Ring me again, or you won't hear about what's happening with Eddie,' she threatened jokingly.

'Will do!' Petra giggled. 'Bye, honeybun.'

Ashley clicked off the call, grabbed Bronte by the collar and opened the front door. This was the first time someone had rung the doorbell since she'd had the dog and it had obviously unsettled her. Picking her up, she straightened to see a tall man standing there. A tall man with a suntan and a familiar wide grin.

'Hi, Ash,' Eddie said. 'So, this is Bronte!'

Chapter Three

'Eddie!' Excitement at seeing him after so long overshot any inhibition and she grabbed him and hugged him tight, the little poodle still in her arms.

'Think something's coming between us, kiddo.' He looked down in alarm. 'And it's growling.'

'I probably squashed her.' Ashley stared at Bronte, stricken. 'Did I squish you, little one? Come on, I'll find you a Bonio.'

'Do I get one too?' Eddie asked, amused.

'Do you eat dog biscuits?' she said over her shoulder. 'Or would you settle for a beer?' He followed her into the sitting room, and she busied herself with the tin of biscuits and settling the dog in her basket. As ever, Eddie's bulk dominated the tiny space, and it made her self-conscious.

'You know what I'd really like?'

'What's that?'

'A cup of good old British tea.'

'I think I can manage that.' Moving into the kitchen, she washed her hands and switched on the kettle. 'When did you get in?'

'Got the red eye into Bristol, headed straight into a

meeting for my show and then drove here.' He yawned hugely. 'Jeez though, flying this direction always knocks me out. Tried to sleep on the plane but I never can.'

She took out two mugs. 'And how's everything at home, with... erm... Bree and the baby?'

He scrubbed an exhausted hand over his eyes. 'Yeah. Okay. All good. Bree's staying with Mom until she feels stronger. Mom's loving having a baby to look after.'

'It must have been awful leaving Hal.'

'It was. Yeah.'

There was something off about his tone but Ashley put it down to jetlag and decided not to pursue the topic just now. Changing gears, she said, 'I've just been speaking to Petra on the phone.'

'Oh? Good. How's she doing?'

While she made the tea, Ashley filled him in on everything Petra had told her. Bringing the tray over to where he was sitting, she put it on the table in front of the sofa and sat on the floor. It reminded her of when Eddie had first called at the flat all those months ago. She recalled the almost instant physical attraction she'd felt to him and smiled. It had been so uncomplicated back then when her only concern had been the speed and intensity of her feelings.

Bronte, having scoffed the biscuit, decided she

wanted to investigate the visitor so jumped onto the sofa and sniffed Eddie.

'Hey there, little one,' he crooned, holding out his hand. 'See, I'm not so scary.' Bronte whickered a little, turned round and stuck her bottom up in the air.

Ashley laughed. 'Believe it or not, that means she likes you.'

Eddie scratched the dog's rump and Bronte, in ecstasies, wiggled round and cuddled into him.

'There you go, friend for life.'

'Feels good to have a dog next to me again.'

'You must miss yours,' Ashley said softly. Eddie's elderly Labrador, Bowie, had been put to sleep a few months previously whilst in Bree's care.

He glanced up, his hazel eyes full of emotion. 'I did. Still do, I guess. Not as much as I've missed you though, Ash.' Bronte, as though sensing his anguish, settled on his lap. As he cuddled the dog, his face was shuttered but Ashley could hear the pain in his voice. 'I really felt for Bree having to make the decision to have him put to sleep. It's a tough enough thing to do for your own dog but when you're looking after someone else's it's even harder.'

'I'm sure she did what she felt she had to.'

'Yeah, I guess.' He shoved an exhausted hand

through his hair, making it untidy. 'It's all been hard, Ash. God knows it's not how I saw me having a child – getting my ex pregnant by accident when we'd split up. I feel constantly torn in two. I was desperate to get back to you, but it was hell leaving Hal.'

'It must have been.' Ashley felt a pang of the familiar jealousy and tried to repress it. She needed to learn to accept baby Hal. 'When are you hoping to get back and see them again?'

He gave her a hard, swift glance. 'See Hal. It's only Hal I want to see, not Bree. And, much as I long to be with my son in the States, this is where I want to be. I want to be with you, Ash, here, in the UK. It's where my work is now.' His eyes flickered with emotion as his gaze intensified. 'It's where my heart is, too.'

This was how her life would be from now on, Ashley thought. If she built a relationship with Eddie, Hal – and to some extent, Bree – would always be there in his life too. And it wouldn't change even once Hal was out of the baby stage. She wondered if it would get slightly easier, though, when Hal was older. He'd be able to stay with his father independently, maybe even come and live in the UK with them. But that all seemed a long way off. A flash of understanding seared her brain. However hard it was for her, it must be doubly so for Eddie. He'd miss so much of his son growing up. Breath snatched in her throat. He was willing to give all that up because he wanted to live in England and to be with her. It was some sacrifice.

'Eddie, I—' she began.

'Ashley, if you don't come over here and kiss me, I'm not going to be responsible for my actions. Get here now. I gotta prove to you it's not Bree I want.'

'But we have things to talk through.'

'Yes, we do,' he agreed wearily. 'But not right now. Right now I just need to hold you. I'm aching to hold you.'

Ashley pulled herself up and slid onto the sofa next to him, which, as always, sagged in the middle and threw them together. Eddie didn't move. She looked directly into his eyes. 'Well,' she said, with a shy smile, 'what are you waiting for? I'm here.'

He groaned, slipped a hand around the back of her neck and pulled her close. Bronte jumped off his lap and slunk to her basket to watch the proceedings with interest. Eddie sank his face into Ashley's hair and inhaled. 'You smell so damn good,' he whispered. 'You always did. Did you know your scent comes to me in my dreams? It haunts me.'

His low voice, pulsing with need, sent thrills running through her body. She shifted closer, resting her head on his shoulder, and they sat close together, content for the moment to simply listen to one another breathe.

After a long time, Ashley asked quietly, 'Did you make any progress with your grandfather's story when you were back home?' Eddie seemed such a huge part of her life now, it was strange to think it was only a few months ago that he'd come to Berecombe to find out more about his GI relative who had been billeted in the town in the months before D-Day. It was how they had come together. She had been planning the funeral for another war hero – a local man, Jimmy Larcombe – and Eddie thought Jimmy might have known his grandfather.

Eddie groaned. 'It's like pulling teeth. So slow! I got through to some guy at the regimental headquarters. He said he'd do the research, send on any paperwork or records he had, but it would take time.'

'I'm sorry.'

'Guess I'm no further forward than I was back in February. I'll just have to wait to see what they come up with.' He shifted away and reached into his pocket. 'I brought this back though. Thought you might like to see it. It's his dog tag. Mom thought I ought to have it. She had it put on a chain if I ever wanted to wear it, but it didn't seem right somehow.' He handed it over.

Ashley took it, the cold links of the chain slithering

between her trembling fingers. It was small, metal and oblong, the letters and numbers worn smooth and almost indecipherable. She didn't think she would be able to wear it either if she was in Eddie's shoes. This had been around a soldier's neck when he'd gone into battle – and in Eddie's grandfather's case, into some of the most brutal fighting of World War Two. 'Fascinating.' She handed it back, shivering a little.

He put it back in his pocket. 'It resonates, doesn't it? Oh, Ash, I'm sorry. I didn't mean to upset you,' he said, seeing the emotion in her eyes. 'Hey, come here. I'm sorry,' he repeated. 'Let's forget about all that.' He hugged her close and then, lifting her chin with the tip of his finger, he outlined her mouth, frowning as he did so, as if trying to commit its shape to memory. Running his hand over her face he traced her eyebrows, the contours of her cheekbones. He found the scar from her accident behind her ear and tipped her head gently sideways to trace it with his lips, his touch so delicate and needy, her breath hitched. His lips trailed over her jaw, remembering the sensitive part of her neck, and his fingers found her collar bone and the swell of her breast. And then he groaned again, and their mouths found one another and they kissed. They were tentative at first, exploring, hardly daring to believe they could, after all this time. Then Ashley flung her arms around his neck and pulled him in close, relishing the weight of him against her. The mood shifted and built into an urgent longing.

Eddie unzipped her jeans and slid his hand under the denim. Ashley's head fell back, her eyes closed as she concentrated on the deliciousness of the skin-on-skin touch. She wanted him so much. Through the hot fug of her need, she pictured them sprawled naked on her bed. Eddie's hand skimmed hotly over her hip. Naked. They'd be naked. She froze. All desire fled.

He picked up on the sudden change in mood instantly. 'Too soon? Too much?' He backed off and gazed into her eyes. 'What's wrong, Ash?' Seeing her distress, he caressed her cheek. 'Hey, baby, what's wrong?'

'I—' She faltered. How could she explain? Especially as she'd shown no such inhibition the time she'd launched herself at him outside the theatre. But she'd had clothes on then.

He sat back, gently tidying her shirt. 'It's too soon for you, isn't it? Maybe we should sit back, take it easy, have that talk. Come here.' He pulled her back to him once more, resting her head on his shoulder, banding his arms around her. Gradually their breathing returned to normal.

'I need to tell you something.'

'Shoot, kiddo. I'm all ears.' His hand stroking her hair soothed.

'I'm ugly, Eddie.'

Don't forget to order your copy of *Blue Skies and Blackberry Pies* to find out what happens next!

ONE MORE CHAPTER

One More Chapter is an award-winning global division of HarperCollins.

Sign up to our newsletter to get our latest eBook deals and stay up to date with our weekly Book Club!
<u>Subscribe here.</u>

Meet the team at
www.onemorechapter.com

Follow us!
 @OneMoreChapter_
 @OneMoreChapter
 @onemorechapterhc

Do you write unputdownable fiction?
We love to hear from new voices.
Find out how to submit your novel at
<u>www.onemorechapter.com/submissions</u>